Eyes of the Cat

Ruskin Bond has been writing for over sixty years, and now has over 120 titles in print—novels, collections of short stories, poetry, essays, anthologies and books for children. His first novel, *The Room on the Roof*, received the prestigious John Llewellyn Rhys Prize in 1957. He has also received the Padma Shri (1999), the Padma Bhushan (2014) and two awards from Sahitya Akademi—one for his short stories and another for his writings for children. In 2012, the Delhi government gave him its Lifetime Achievement Award.

Born in 1934, Ruskin Bond grew up in Jamnagar, Shimla, New Delhi and Dehradun. Apart from three years in the UK, he has spent all his life in India, and now lives in Mussoorie with his adopted family.

Eyes of the Cat

Selected and Compiled by
RUSKIN BOND

RUPA

Published by
Rupa Publications India Pvt. Ltd 2017
7/16, Ansari Road, Daryaganj
New Delhi 110002

Sales centres:
Allahabad Bengaluru Chennai
Hyderabad Jaipur Kathmandu
Kolkata Mumbai

Copyright © Ruskin Bond 2017

This is a work of fiction. Names, characters, places and incidents are either the product of the author's imagination or are used fictitiously and any resemblance to any actual person, living or dead, events or locales is entirely coincidental.

All rights reserved.
No part of this publication may be reproduced, transmitted, or stored in a retrieval system, in any form or by any means, electronic, mechanical, photocopying, recording or otherwise, without the prior permission of the publisher.

ISBN: 978-81-291-4804-9

First impression 2017

10 9 8 7 6 5 4 3 2 1

Printed at Thomson Press India Ltd., Faridabad

This book is sold subject to the condition that it shall not, by way of trade or otherwise, be lent, resold, hired out, or otherwise circulated, without the publisher's prior consent, in any form of binding or cover other than that in which it is published.

CONTENTS

Introduction	vii
A Horseman in the Sky *Ambrose Bierce*	1
The Princess and the Puma *O. Henry*	9
The Hand *Guy de Maupassant*	17
The Story of B 24 *Arthur Conan Doyle*	25
The Tell-Tale Heart *Edgar Allan Poe*	44
The Magic Shop *H.G. Wells*	51
The Signal-Man *Charles Dickens*	65
Désirée's Baby *Kate Chopin*	82
The Vampire *Sydney Horler*	90

Eyes of the Cat *Ruskin Bond*	97
The Statement of Randolph Carter *H.P. Lovecraft*	100
The Story of Muhammad Din *Rudyard Kipling*	108
Night of the Millennium *Ruskin Bond*	113

INTRODUCTION

As far as short stories go, it's difficult to say what is 'short' exactly. Anything that is below 15,000 words could be a short story. Reading a long short story gives the satisfaction of not having to wade through a novel and being able to reach the end fairly soon, while for the writer it gives some space to build the characters and the plot. But any story that is about 2,000 words or a bit more, makes not only for a quick read, but the writer too needs to tell the story at a fast pace without sounding hurried or compromising on the details.

There are stories that along with being short, also come with a hint of the macabre and the supernatural and have a twist in the ending. This collection contains a few such stories that tick all these boxes. Some are short and snappy. Others have supernatural happenings. And yet some others have a twisted ending. And there are a few that combine all of these!

O. Henry's story 'The Princess and the Puma' is a wonderful example of the supremely satisfying short story. The princess who can look after herself in the wild and the man who thinks it is he who can do all the hunting and protecting is wryly funny. For the macabre, there is the old favourite Guy de Maupassant. His story 'The Hand' is unlikely to be forgotten in a hurry with its gruesome details of a severed hand that has yet some life in it. Then there is Edgar Allan Poe. His dark and fiendish stories are always a treat to read. Here you will find 'The Tell-Tale Heart', and it's enough to say that when Poe writes about the heart, he is not writing about romantic matters of the heart but of something of the muscle and tissue filled real heart. Can the beating sound of a dead man's heart give away the identity of the murderer?

I could not resist including here another writer I have admired—H. G. Wells. He was, of course, most renowned for his science fiction—*The Time Machine* and *The Invisible Man*, among others. Here we have one of his short stories, 'The Magic Shop', and it is full of surprises like his longer works. 'Désirée's Baby' brings in a completely different flavour from the rest. It is not about the twisted ending or the supernatural here. It is about the prejudices of the human race and how we have within us the capability to hate and despise, as much as we have the ability to love and care.

Rudyard Kipling, H.P. Lovecraft are some of the other writers whose stories you will find in this collection. Kipling started his writing as a journalist. Some of his early writings were for the *Civil and Military Gazette*, from Lahore, and were written keeping in mind the limited column space available.

I wrote the story 'Eyes of the Cat' because a young reader had asked me to write something frightening. She was moderately pleased with the result when she read the story. I present it here again, and hope many others will read and enjoy it.

Ruskin Bond

A HORSEMAN IN THE SKY

Ambrose Bierce

One sunny afternoon in the autumn of the year 1861, a soldier lay in a clump of laurel by the side of a road in Western Virginia. He lay at full length, upon his stomach, his feet resting upon the toes, his head upon the left forearm. His extended right hand loosely grasped his rifle. But for the somewhat methodical disposition of his limbs and a slight rhythmic movement of the cartridge-box at the back of his belt, he might have been thought to be dead. He was asleep at his post of duty. But if detected he would be dead shortly afterward, that being the just and legal penalty of his crime.

The clump of laurel in which the criminal lay was in the angle of a road which, after ascending southward, a steep acclivity to that point, turned sharply to the west, running along the summit for perhaps one hundred yards. There it turned southward again and went zigzagging downward through the forest. At the salient of that second angle was a large flat rock, jutting out from the ridge to the northward, overlooking the deep valley from which the road ascended. The rock capped a high cliff; a stone dropped from its outer edge would have fallen sheer downward 1,000 feet to the tops of the pines. The angle where the soldier lay was on another spur of the same cliff. Had he been awake he would have commanded a view, not only of the short arm of the road and the jutting rock but of the entire profile of the cliff below it. It might well have made him giddy to look.

The country was wooded everywhere except at the bottom of the valley to the northward, where there was a small natural meadow, through which flowed a stream scarcely visible from the valley's rim. This open ground looked hardly larger than an ordinary dooryard, but was really several acres in extent. Its green was more vivid than that of the enclosing forest. Away beyond it rose a line of giant cliffs similar to those upon which we are supposed to stand in our survey of the savage scene, and through which the road had somehow made its climb to the summit. The configuration of the valley, indeed, was such that from out point of observation it seemed entirely shut in, and one could not but have wondered how the road which found a way out of it had found a way into it, and whence came and whither went the waters of the stream that parted the meadow 2,000 feet below.

No country is so wild and difficult but men will make it a theatre of war; concealed in the forest at the bottom of that military rat-trap, in which half a hundred men in possession of the exits might have starved an army to submission, lay five regiments of Federal infantry. They had marched all the previous day and night and were resting. At nightfall they would take to the road again, climb to the place where their unfaithful sentinel now slept, and, descending the other slope of the ridge, fall upon a camp of the enemy at about midnight. Their hope was to surprise it, for the road led to the rear of it. In case of failure their position would be perilous in the extreme; and fail they surely would should accident or vigilance apprise the enemy of their movement.

The sleeping sentinel in the clump of laurel was a young Virginian named Carter Druse. He was the son of wealthy parents, an only child, and had known such ease and cultivation and high living as wealth and taste were able to command in the mountain country of Western Virginia. His home was but a few miles from where he now lay. One morning he had risen from the breakfast table and said, quietly and gravely: 'Father, a Union regiment has arrived at Grafton. I am going to join it.'

The father lifted his leonine head, looked at the son a moment in silence, and replied: 'Go, Carter, and, whatever may occur, do what you conceive to be your duty. Virginia, to which you are a traitor, must get on without you. Should we both live to the end of the war, we will speak further of the matter. Your mother, as the physician has informed you, is in a most critical condition; at the best she cannot be with us longer than a few weeks, but that time is precious. It would be better not to disturb her.'

So Carter Druse, bowing reverently to his father, who returned the salute with a stately courtesy which masked a breaking heart, left the home of his childhood to go soldiering. By conscience and courage, by deeds of devotion and daring, he soon commended himself to his fellows and his officers; and it was to these qualities and to some knowledge of the country that he owed his selection for his present perilous duty at the extreme outpost. Nevertheless, fatigue had been stronger than resolution, and he had fallen asleep. What good or bad angel came in a dream to rouse him from his state of crime who shall say? Without a movement, without a sound, in the profound silence and the languor of the late afternoon, some invisible messenger of fate touched with unsealing finger the eyes of his consciousness—whispered into the ear of his spirit the mysterious awakening word which no human lips have ever spoken, no human memory ever has recalled. He quietly raised his forehead from his arm and looked between the masking stems of the laurels, instinctively closing his right hand about the stock of his rifle.

His first feeling was a keen artistic delight. On a colossal pedestal, the cliff, motionless at the extreme edge of the capping rock and sharply outlined against the sky, was an equestrian statue of impressive dignity. The figure of the man sat on the figure of the horse, straight and soldierly, but with the repose of a Grecian god carved in the marble which limits the suggestion of activity. The grey costume harmonized with its aerial background; the metal of accoutrement and caparison was softened and subdued by the shadow; the animal's skin had no points of highlight. A carbine, strikingly foreshortened, lay across the pommel of the saddle, kept in place by the right hand grasping it at the 'grip'; the left hand, holding the bridle rein, was invisible. In silhouette against the sky, the profile of the horse was cut with the sharpness of a cameo; it looked across the heights of air to the confronting cliffs beyond. The face of the rider, turned slightly to the left, showed only an outline of temple and beard; he was looking downward to the bottom of the valley. Magnified by its lift against the sky and by the soldier's testifying sense of the formidableness of a near enemy, the group appeared of heroic, almost colossal, size.

For an instant Druse had a strange, half-defined feeling that he had slept to the end of the war and was looking upon a noble work of art reared upon that commanding eminence to commemorate the deeds of a heroic past of which he had been an inglorious part. The feeling was dispelled by a slight movement of the group; the horse, without moving its feet, had drawn its body slightly backward from the verge; the man remained immobile as before. Broad awake and keenly alive to the significance of the situation, Druse now brought the butt of his rifle against his cheek by cautiously pushing the barrel forward through the bushes, cocked the piece, and, glancing through the sights, covered a vital spot of the horseman's breast. A touch upon the trigger and all would have been well with Carter Druse. At that instant the horseman turned his head and looked in the direction of his concealed foeman—seemed to look into his very face, into his eyes, into his brave compassionate heart.

Is it, then, so terrible to kill an enemy in war—an enemy who has surprised a secret vital to the safety of oneself and comrades—an enemy more formidable for his knowledge than all his army for its numbers? Carter Druse grew deathly pale; he shook in every limb, turned faint, and saw the statuesque group before him as black figures, rising, falling, moving unsteadily in arcs of circles in a fiery sky. His hand fell away from his weapon, his head slowly dropped until his face rested on the leaves in which he lay. This courageous gentleman and hardy soldier was near swooning from intensity of emotion.

It was not for long; in another moment his face was raised from earth, his hands resumed their places on the rifle, his forefinger sought the trigger; mind, heart, and eyes were clear, conscience and reason sound. He could not hope to capture that enemy; to alarm him would but send him dashing to his camp with his fatal news. The duty of the soldier was plain: the man must be shot dead from ambush—without warning, without a moment's spiritual preparation, with never so much as an unspoken prayer, he must be sent to his account. But no—there is a hope; he may have discovered nothing—perhaps he is but admiring the sublimity of the landscape. If permitted, he may turn and ride carelessly away in the direction whence he came. Surely it will be possible to judge at the instant of his withdrawing whether he knows. It may well be that his fixity of attention— Druse turned his head and looked below, through the deeps of air downward, as from the surface to the bottom of a translucent sea. He saw creeping across the green meadow a sinuous line of figures of men and horses—some foolish commander was permitting the soldiers of his escort to water their beasts in the open, in plain view from a hundred summits!

Druse withdrew his eyes from the valley and fixed them again upon the group of man and horse in the sky, and again it was through the sights of his rifle. But this time his aim was at the horse. In his memory, as if they were a divine mandate, rang the words of his father at their parting: 'Whatever may occur, do what you conceive to be your duty.' He was calm now. His teeth were firmly but not rigidly closed; his nerves were as tranquil as a sleeping babe's—not a tremor affected any muscle of his body; his breathing, until suspended in the act of taking aim, was regular and slow. Duty had conquered; the spirit had said to the body: 'Peace, be still.' He fired.

At that moment an officer of the Federal force, who, in a spirit of adventure or in quest of knowledge, had left the hidden bivouac in the valley, and, with aimless feet, had made his way to the lower edge of a small open space near the foot of the cliff, was considering what he had to gain by pushing his exploration farther. At a distance of a quarter mile before him, but apparently at a stone's throw, rose from its fringe of pines the gigantic face of rock, towering to so great a height above him that it made him giddy to look up to where its edge cut a sharp, rugged line against the sky. At some distance away to his right it presented a clean, vertical profile against a background of blue sky to a point half of the way down, and of distant hills hardly less blue thence to the tops of the trees at its base. Lifting his eyes to the dizzy altitude of its summit, the officer saw an astonishing sight—a man on horseback riding down into the valley through the air!

Straight upright sat the rider, in military fashion, with a firm seat in the saddle, a strong clutch upon the rein to hold his charger from too impetuous a plunge. From his bare head his long hair streamed upward, waving like a plume. His right hand was concealed in the cloud of the horse's lifted mane. The animal's body was as level as if every hoof-stroke encountered the resistant earth. Its motions were those of a wild gallop, but even as the officer looked they ceased, with all the legs thrown sharply forward as in the act of alighting from a leap. But this was a flight!

Filled with amazement and terror by this apparition of a horseman in the sky—half believing himself the chosen scribe of some new Apocalypse, the officer was overcome by the intensity of his emotions; his legs failed him and he fell. Almost at the same instant he heard a crashing sound in the trees—a sound that died without an echo, and all was still.

The officer rose to his feet, trembling. The familiar sensation of an abraded shin recalled his dazed faculties. Pulling himself together, he ran rapidly obliquely away from the cliff to a point a half mile from its foot; thereabout he expected to find his man; and thereabout he naturally failed. In the fleeting instant of his vision his imagination had been so wrought upon by the apparent grace and ease and intention of the marvellous performance that it did not occur to him that the line of march of aerial cavalry is directed downward, and that he could find the objects of his search at the very foot of the cliff. A half hour later he returned to camp.

This officer was a wise man; he knew better than to tell an incredible truth. He said nothing of what he had seen. But when the commander asked him if in his scout he had learned anything of advantage to the expedition, he answered:

'Yes, sir; there is no road leading down into this valley from the southward.'

The commander, knowing better, smiled.

After firing his shot Private Carter Druse reloaded his rifle and resumed his watch. Ten minutes had hardly passed when a Federal sergeant crept cautiously to him on hands and knees. Druse neither turned his head nor looked at him, but lay without motion or sign of recognition.

'Did you fire?' the sergeant whispered.

'Yes.'

'At what?'

'A horse. It was standing on yonder rock—pretty far out. You see it is no longer there. It went over the cliff.'

The man's face was white, but he showed no other sign of emotion. Having answered, he turned away his face and said no more. The sergeant did not understand.

'See here, Druse,' he said, after a moment's silence, 'it's no use making a mystery. I order you to report. Was there anybody on the horse?'

'Yes.'

'Who?'

'My father.'

The sergeant rose to his feet and walked away. 'Good God!' he said.

THE PRINCESS AND THE PUMA

O. Henry

There had to be a king and queen, of course. The king was a terrible old man who wore six-shooters and spurs, and shouted in such a tremendous voice that the rattlers on the prairie would run into their holes under the prickly pear. Before there was a royal family they called the man 'Whispering Ben'. When he came to own 50,000 acres of land and more cattle than he could count, they called him O'Donnell 'the Cattle King'.

The queen had been a Mexican girl from Laredo. She made a good, mild, Colorado claro wife, and even succeeded in teaching Ben to modify his voice sufficiently while in the house to keep the dishes from being broken. When Ben got to be king, she would sit on the gallery of Espinosa Ranch and weave rush mats. When wealth became so irresistible and oppressive that upholstered chairs and a centre table were brought down from San Antone in wagons, she bowed her smooth, dark head, and shared the fate of Danaë.

To avoid *lèse-majesté* you have been presented first to the king and queen. They do not enter the story, which might be called 'The Chronicle of the Princess, the Happy Thought, and the Lion that Bungled his Job.'

Josefa O'Donnell was the surviving daughter, the princess. From her mother she inherited warmth of nature and a dusky, semi-tropic beauty. From Ben O'Donnell the royal she acquired a store in intrepidity, common sense, and the faculty of ruling. The combination was worth going miles to see. Josefa while riding her pony at a gallop could put five out of six bullets through a tomato-can swinging at the end of a string. She could play for hours with a white kitten she owned, dressing it in all manner of absurd clothes. Scorning a pencil, she could tell you out of her head what 1545 two-year-olds would bring on the hoof, at $8.50 per head. Roughly speaking, the Espinosal Ranch is forty miles long and thirty broad—but mostly on leased land. Josefa, on her pony, had prospected over every mile of it. Every cow-puncher on the range knew her by sight and was a loyal vassal. Ripley Givens, foreman of one of the Espinosal outfits, saw her one day, and made up his mind to form a royal matrimonial alliance. Presumptuous? No. In those days in the Nueces country a man was a man. And, after all, the title of cattle king does not presuppose blood royal. Often it only signifies that its owner wears the crown in token of his magnificent qualities in the art of cattle stealing.

One day Ripley Givens rode over to the Double Elm Ranch to inquire about a bunch of strayed yearlings. He was late in setting out on his return trip, and it was sundown when he struck the White Horse Crossing of the Nueces. From there to his own camp it was sixteen miles. To the Espinosal ranch house it was twelve. Givens was tired. He decided to pass the night at the Crossing.

There was a fine waterhole in the riverbed. The banks were thickly covered with great trees, undergrown with brush. Back from the waterhole fifty yards was a stretch of curly mesquite grass—supper for his horse and bed for himself. Givens staked his horse, and spread out his saddle blankets to dry. He sat down with his back against a tree and rolled a cigarette. From somewhere in the dense timber along the river came a sudden, rageful, shivering wail. The pony danced at the end of his rope and blew a whistling snort of comprehending fear. Givens puffed at his cigarette, but he reached leisurely for his pistol-belt, which lay on the grass, and twirled the cylinder of his weapon tentatively. A great gar plunged with a loud splash into the waterhole. A little brown rabbit skipped around a bunch of catclaw and sat twitching his whiskers and looking humorously at Givens. The pony went on eating grass.

It is well to be reasonably watchful when a Mexican lion sings soprano along the arroyos at sundown. The burden of his song may be that young calves and fat lambs are scarce, and that he has a carnivorous desire for your acquaintance.

In the grass lay an empty fruit can, cast there by some former sojourner. Givens caught sight of it with a grunt of satisfaction. In his coat pocket tied behind his saddle was a handful or two of ground coffee. Black coffee and cigarettes! What ranchero could desire more?

In two minutes he had a little fire going clearly. He started, with his can, for the waterhole. When within fifteen yards of its edge he saw, between the bushes, a side-saddled pony with down-dropped reins cropping grass a little distance to his left. Just rising from her hands and knees on the brink of the waterhole was Josefa O'Donnell. She had been drinking water, and she brushed the sand from the palms of her hands. Ten yards away, to her right, half concealed by a clump of sacuista, Givens saw the crouching form of the Mexican lion. His amber eyelids glared hungrily; six feet from them was the tip of the tail stretched straight, like a pointer's. His hind-quarters rocked with the motion of the cat tribe preliminary to leaping.

Givens did what he could. His six-shooter was thirty-five yards away lying on the grass. He gave a loud yell, and dashed between the lion and the princess.

The 'rucus,' as Givens called it afterward, was brief and somewhat confused. When he arrived on the line of attack he saw a dim streak in the air, and heard a couple of faint cracks. Then a hundred pounds of Mexican lion plumped down upon his head and flattened him, with a heavy jar, to the ground. He remembered calling out: 'Let up, now—no fair gouging!' and then he crawled from under the lion like a worm, with his mouth full of grass and dirt, and a big lump on the back of his head where it had struck the root of a water elm. The lion lay motionless. Givens, feeling aggrieved, and suspicious of fouls, shook his fist at the lion, and shouted: 'I'll wrestle you again for twenty—' and then he got back to himself.

Josefa was standing in her tracks, quietly reloading her silver-mounted .38. It had not been a difficult shot. The lion's head made an easier mark than a tomato-can swinging at the end of a string. There was a provoking, teasing, maddening smile upon her mouth and in her dark eyes. The would-be-rescuing knight felt the fire of his fiasco burn down to his soul. Here had been his chance, the chance that he had dreamed of; and Momus, and not Cupid, had presided over it. The satyrs in the wood were, no doubt, holding their sides in hilarious, silent laughter. There had been something like vaudeville—say Signor Givens and his funny knockabout act with the stuffed lion.

'Is that you, Mr Givens?' said Josefa, in her deliberate, saccharine contralto. 'You nearly spoiled my shot when you yelled. Did you hurt your head when you fell?'

'Oh, no,' said Givens, quietly; 'that didn't hurt.' He stooped ignominiously and dragged his best Stetson hat from under the beast. It was crushed and wrinkled to a fine comedy effect. Then he knelt down and softly stroked the fierce, open-jawed head of the dead lion.

'Poor old Bill!' he exclaimed, mournfully.

'What's that?' asked Josefa, sharply.

'Of course you didn't know, Miss Josefa,' said Givens, with an air of one allowing magnanimity to triumph over grief. 'Nobody can blame you. I tried to save him, but I couldn't let you know in time.'

'Save who?'

'Why, Bill. I've been looking for him all day. You see, he's been our camp pet for two years. Poor old fellow, he wouldn't have hurt a cottontail rabbit. It'll break the boys all up when they hear about it. But you couldn't tell, of course, that Bill was just trying to play with you.'

Josefa's black eyes burned steadily upon him. Ripley Givens met the test successfully. He stood rumpling the yellow-brown curls on his head pensively. In his eyes was regret, not unmingled with a gentle reproach. His smooth features were set to a pattern of indisputable sorrow. Josefa wavered.

'What was your pet doing here?' she asked, making a last stand. 'There's no camp near the White Horse Crossing.'

'The old rascal ran away from camp yesterday,' answered Givens, readily. 'It's a wonder the coyotes didn't scare him to death. You see, Jim Webster, our horse wrangler, brought a little terrier pup into camp last week. The pup made life miserable for Bill—he used to chase him around and chew his hind legs for hours at a time. Every night when bedtime came Bill would sneak under one of the boys' blankets and sleep to keep the pup from finding him. I reckon he must have been worried pretty desperate or he wouldn't have run away. He was always afraid to get out of sight of camp.'

Josefa looked at the body of the fierce animal. Givens gently patted one of the formidable paws that could have killed a yearling calf with one blow. Slowly a red flush widened upon the dark olive face of the girl. Was it the signal of shame of the true sportsman who has brought down ignoble quarry? Her eyes grew softer, and the lowered lids drove away all their bright mockery.

'I'm very sorry,' she said, humbly; 'but he looked so big, and jumped so high that—'

'Poor old Bill was hungry,' interrupted Givens, in quick defence of the deceased. 'We always made him jump for his supper in camp. He would lie down and roll over for a piece of meat. When he saw you he thought he was going to get something to eat from you.'

Suddenly Josefa's eyes opened wide.

'I might have shot you!' she exclaimed. 'You ran right in between. You risked your life to save your pet! That was fine, Mr Givens. I like a man who is kind to animals.'

Yes; there was even admiration in her gaze now. After all, there was a hero rising out of the ruins of the anti-climax. The look on Givens's face would have secured him a high position in the S.P.C.A.

'I always loved 'em,' said he; 'horses, dogs, Mexican lions, cows, alligators—'

'I hate alligators,' instantly demurred Josefa; 'crawly, muddy things!'

'Did I say alligators?' said Givens. 'I meant antelopes, of course.'

Josefa's conscience drove her to make further amends. She held out her hand penitently. There was a bright, unshed drop in each of her eyes.

'Please forgive me, Mr Givens, won't you? I'm only a girl, you know, and I was frightened at first. I'm very, very sorry I shot Bill. You don't know how ashamed I feel. I wouldn't have done it for anything.'

Givens took the proffered hand. He held it for a time while he allowed the generosity of his nature to overcome his grief at the loss of Bill. At last it was clear that he had forgiven her.

'Please don't speak of it any more, Miss Josefa. 'Twas enough to frighten any young lady the way Bill looked. I'll explain it all right to the boys.'

'Are you really sure you don't hate me?' Josefa came closer to him impulsively. Her eyes were sweet—oh, sweet and pleading with gracious penitence. 'I would hate any one who would kill my kitten. And how daring and kind of you to risk being shot when you tried to save him! How very few men would have done that!' Victory wrested from defeat! Vaudeville turned into drama! Bravo, Ripley Givens!

It was now twilight. Of course Miss Josefa could not be allowed to ride on to the ranch house alone. Givens resaddled his pony in spite of that animal's reproachful glances, and rode with her. Side by side they galloped across the smooth grass, the princess and the man who was kind to animals. The prairie odours of fruitful earth and delicate bloom were thick and sweet around them. Coyotes yelping over there on the hill! No fear. And yet—

Josefa rode closer. A little hand seemed to grope. Givens found it with his own. The ponies kept an even gait. The hands lingered together, and the owner of one explained.

'I never was frightened before, but just think! How terrible it would be to meet a really wild lion! Poor Bill! I'm so glad you came with me!'

O'Donnell was sitting on the ranch gallery.

'Hello, Rip!' he shouted—'that you?'

'He rode in with me,' said Josefa. 'I lost my way and was late.'

'Much obliged,' called the cattle king. 'Stop over, Rip, and ride to camp in the morning.'

But Givens would not. He would push on to camp. There was a bunch of steers to start off on the trail at daybreak. He said goodnight, and trotted away.

An hour later, when the lights were out, Josefa, in her nightrobe, came to her door and called to the king in his own room across the brick-paved hallway:

'Say, Pop, you know that old Mexican lion they call the 'Gotch-eared Devil'—the one that killed Gonzales, Mr Martin's sheep herder, and about fifty calves on the Salada range? Well, I settled his hash this afternoon over at the White Horse Crossing. Put two balls in his head with my .38 while he was on the jump. I knew him by the slice gone from his left ear that old Gonzales cut off with his machete. You couldn't have made a better shot yourself, Daddy.'

'Bully for you!' thundered Whispering Ben from the darkness of the royal chamber.

THE HAND

Guy de Maupassant

All were crowding around M. Bermutier, the judge, who was giving his opinion about the Saint-Cloud mystery. For a month this inexplicable crime had been the talk of Paris. Nobody could make head or tail of it.

M. Bermutier, standing with his back to the fireplace, was talking, citing the evidence, discussing the various theories, but arriving at no conclusion.

Some women had risen, in order to get nearer to him, and were standing with their eyes fastened on the clean-shaven face of the judge, who was saying such weighty things. They, were shaking and trembling, moved by fear and curiosity, and by the eager and insatiable desire for the horrible, which haunts the soul of every woman. One of them, paler than the others, said during a pause:

'It's terrible. It verges on the supernatural. The truth will never be known.'

The judge turned to her:

'True, madame, it is likely that the actual facts will never be discovered. As for the word 'supernatural' which you have just used, it has nothing to do with the matter. We are in the presence of a very cleverly conceived and executed crime, so well enshrouded in mystery that we cannot disentangle it from the involved circumstances which surround it. But once I had to take charge of an affair in which the uncanny seemed to play a part. In fact, the case became so confusing that it had to be given up.'

Several women exclaimed at once:

'Oh! Tell us about it!'

M. Bermutier smiled in a dignified manner, as a judge should, and went on:

'Do not think, however, that I, for one minute, ascribed anything in the case to supernatural influences. I believe only in normal causes. But if, instead of using the word 'supernatural' to express what we do not understand, we were simply to make use of the word 'inexplicable,' it would be much better. At any rate, in the affair of which I am about to tell you, it is especially the surrounding, preliminary circumstances which impressed me. Here are the facts:

'I was, at that time, a judge at Ajaccio, a little white city on the edge of a bay which is surrounded by high mountains.

'The majority of the cases which came up before me concerned vendettas. There are some that are superb, dramatic, ferocious, heroic. We find there the most beautiful causes for revenge of which one could dream, enmities hundreds of years old, quieted for a time but never extinguished; abominable stratagems, murders becoming massacres and almost deeds of glory. For two years I heard of nothing but the price of blood, of this terrible Corsican prejudice which compels revenge for insults meted out to the offending person and all his descendants and relatives. I had seen old men, children, cousins murdered; my head was full of these stories.

'One day I learned that an Englishman had just hired a little villa at the end of the bay for several years. He had brought with him a French servant, whom he had engaged on the way at Marseilles.

'Soon this peculiar person, living alone, only going out to hunt and fish, aroused a widespread interest. He never spoke to any one, never went to the town, and every morning he would practice for an hour or so with his revolver and rifle.

'Legends were built up around him. It was said that he was some high personage, fleeing from his fatherland for political reasons; then it was affirmed that he was in hiding after having committed some abominable crime. Some particularly horrible circumstances were even mentioned.

'In my judicial position I thought it necessary to get some information about this man, but it was impossible to learn anything. He called himself Sir John Rowell.

'I therefore had to be satisfied with watching him as closely as I could, but I could see nothing suspicious about his actions.

'However, as rumours about him were growing and becoming more widespread, I decided to try to see this stranger myself, and I began to hunt regularly in the neighbourhood of his grounds.

'For a long time I watched without finding an opportunity. At last it came to me in the shape of a partridge which I shot and killed right in front of the Englishman. My dog fetched it for me, but, taking the bird, I went at once to Sir John Rowell and, begging his pardon, asked him to accept it.

'He was a big man, with red hair and beard, very tall, very broad, a kind of calm and polite Hercules. He had nothing of the so-called British stiffness, and in a broad English accent he thanked me warmly for my attention. At the end of a month we had had five or six conversations.

'One night, at last, as I was passing before his door, I saw him in the garden, seated astride a chair, smoking his pipe. I bowed and he invited me to come in and have a glass of beer. I needed no urging.

'He received me with the most punctilious English courtesy, sang the praises of France and of Corsica, and declared that he was quite in love with this country.

'Then, with great caution and under the guise of a vivid interest, I asked him a few questions about his life and his plans. He answered without embarrassment, telling me that he had travelled a great deal in Africa, in the Indies, in America. He added, laughing:

'"I have had many adventures.'

'Then I turned the conversation on hunting, and he gave me the most curious details on hunting the hippopotamus, the tiger, the elephant and even the gorilla.

'I said:

'"Are all these animals dangerous?'

'He smiled:

'"Oh, no! Man is the worst.'

'And he laughed a good broad laugh, the wholesome laugh of a contented Englishman.

'"I have also frequently been man-hunting.'

'Then he began to talk about weapons, and he invited me to come in and see different makes of guns.

'His parlour was draped in black, black silk embroidered in gold. Big yellow flowers, as brilliant as fire, were worked on the dark material.

'He said:

'"It is a Japanese material.'

'But in the middle of the widest panel a strange thing attracted my attention. A black object stood out against a square of red velvet. I went up to it; it was a hand, a human hand. Not the clean white hand of a skeleton, but a dried black hand, with yellow nails, the muscles exposed and traces of old blood on the bones, which were cut off as clean as though it had been chopped off with an axe, near the middle of the forearm.

'Around the wrist, an enormous iron chain, riveted and soldered to this unclean member, fastened it to the wall by a ring, strong enough to hold an elephant in leash.

'I asked:

'"What is that?"

'The Englishman answered quietly:

'"That is my best enemy. It comes from America, too. The bones were severed by a sword and the skin cut off with a sharp stone and dried in the sun for a week.'

'I touched these human remains, which must have belonged to a giant. The uncommonly long fingers were attached by enormous tendons which still had pieces of skin hanging to them in places. This hand was terrible to see; it made one think of some savage vengeance.

'I said:

'"This man must have been very strong."

'The Englishman answered quietly:

'"Yes, but I was stronger than he. I put on this chain to hold him."

'I thought that he was joking. I said:

'"This chain is useless now, the hand won't run away."

'Sir John Rowell answered seriously:

'"It always wants to go away. This chain is needed."'

'I glanced at him quickly, questioning his face, and I asked myself:

'"Is he an insane man or a practical joker?"

'But his face remained inscrutable, calm and friendly. I turned to other subjects, and admired his rifles.

'However, I noticed that he kept three loaded revolvers in the room, as though constantly in fear of some attack.

'I paid him several calls. Then I did not go any more. People had become used to his presence; everybody had lost interest in him.

'A whole year rolled by. One morning, toward the end of November, my servant awoke me and announced that Sir John Rowell had been murdered during the night.

'Half an hour later I entered the Englishman's house, together with the police commissioner and the captain of the gendarmes. The servant, bewildered and in despair, was crying before the door. At first I suspected this man, but he was innocent.

'The guilty party could never be found.

'On entering Sir John's parlour, I noticed the body, stretched out on its back, in the middle of the room.

'His vest was torn, the sleeve of his jacket had been pulled off, everything pointed to a violent struggle.

'The Englishman had been strangled! His face was black, swollen and frightful, and seemed to express a terrible fear. He held something between his teeth, and his neck, pierced by five or six holes which looked as though they had been made by some iron instrument, was covered with blood.

'A physician joined us. He examined the finger marks on the neck for a long time and then made this strange announcement:

'"It looks as though he had been strangled by a skeleton."

'A cold chill seemed to run down my back, and I looked over to where I had formerly seen the terrible hand. It was no longer there. The chain was hanging down, broken.

'I bent over the dead man and, in his contracted mouth, I found one of the fingers of this vanished hand, cut—or rather sawed off by the teeth down to the second knuckle.

'Then the investigation began. Nothing could be discovered. No door, window or piece of furniture had been forced. The two watch dogs had not been aroused from their sleep.

'Here, in a few words, is the testimony of the servant:

'For a month his master had seemed excited. He had received many letters, which he would immediately burn.

'Often, in a fit of passion which approached madness, he had taken a switch and struck wildly at this dried hand riveted to the wall, and which had disappeared, no one knows how, at the very hour of the crime.

'He would go to bed very late and carefully lock himself in. He always kept weapons within reach. Often at night he would talk loudly, as though he were quarrelling with someone.

'That night, somehow, he had made no noise, and it was only on going to open the windows that the servant had found Sir John murdered. He suspected no one.

'I communicated what I knew of the dead man to the judges and public officials. Throughout the whole island a minute investigation was carried on. Nothing could be found out.

'One night, about three months after the crime, I had a terrible nightmare. I seemed to see the horrible hand running over my curtains and walls like an immense scorpion or spider. Three times I awoke, three times I went to sleep again; three times I saw the hideous object galloping round my room and moving its fingers like legs.

'The following day the hand was brought to me, found in the cemetery, on the grave of Sir John Rowell, who had been buried there because we had been unable to find his family. The first finger was missing.

'Ladies, there is my story. I know nothing more.'

The women, deeply stirred, were pale and trembling. One of them exclaimed:

'But that is neither a climax nor an explanation! We will be unable to sleep unless you give us your opinion of what had occurred.'

The judge smiled severely:

'Oh! Ladies, I shall certainly spoil your terrible dreams. I simply believe that the legitimate owner of the hand was not dead, that he came to get it with his remaining one. But I don't know how. It was a kind of vendetta.'

One of the women murmured:

'No, it can't be that.'

And the judge, still smiling, said:

'Didn't I tell you that my explanation would not satisfy you?'

THE STORY OF B 24

Arthur Conan Doyle

I told my story when I was taken, and no one would listen to me. Then I told it again at the trial—the whole thing absolutely as it happened, without so much as a word added. I set it all out truly, so help me God, all that Lady Mannering said and did, and then all that I had said and done, just as it occurred. And what did I get for it? The prisoner put forward a rambling and inconsequential statement, incredible in its details, and unsupported by any shred of corroborative evidence. That was what one of the London papers said, and others let it pass as if I had made no defence at all. And yet, with my own eyes I saw Lord Mannering murdered, and I am as guiltless of it as any man on the jury that tried me.

Now, sir, you are there to receive the petitions of prisoners. It all lies with you. All I ask is that you read it—just read it—and then that you make an inquiry or two about the private character of this Lady Mannering, if she still keeps the name that she had three years ago, when to my sorrow and ruin I came to meet her. You could use a private inquiry agent or a good lawyer, and you would soon learn enough to show you that my story is the true one. Think of the glory it would be to you to have all the papers saying that there would have been a shocking miscarriage of justice if it had not been for your perseverance and intelligence! That must be your reward, since I am a poor man and can offer you nothing. But if you don't do it, may you never lie easy in your bed again! May no night pass that you are not haunted by the thought of the man who rots in gaol because you have not done the duty which you are paid to do! But you will do it, sir, I know. Just make one or two inquiries, and you will soon find which way the wind blows. Remember, also, that the only person who profited by the crime was herself, since it changed her from an unhappy wife to a rich young widow. There's the end of the string in your hand, and you only have to follow it up and see where it leads to.

Mind you, sir, I make no complaint as far as the burglary goes. I don't whine about what I have deserved, and so far I have had no more than I have deserved. Burglary it was, right enough, and my three years have gone to pay for it. It was shown at the trial that I had had a hand in the Merton Cross business, and did a year for that, so my story had the less attention on that account. A man with a previous conviction never gets a really fair trial. I own to the burglary, but when it comes to the murder which brought me a lifer—any judge but Sir James might have given me the gallows—then I tell you that I had nothing to do with it, and that I am an innocent man. And now I'll take you to that night, 13 September 1894, and I'll give you just exactly what occurred, and may God's hand strike me down if I go one inch over the truth.

I had been at Bristol in the summer looking for work, and then I had a notion that I might get something at Portsmouth, for I was trained as a skilled mechanic, so I came tramping my way across the south of England, and doing odd jobs as I went. I was trying all I knew to keep off the cross, for I had done a year in Exeter Gaol, and I had had enough of visiting Queen Victoria. But it's cruel hard to get work when once the black mark is against your name, and it was all I could do to keep soul and body together. At last, after ten days of wood-cutting and stone-breaking on starvation pay, I found myself near Salisbury with a couple of shillings in my pocket, and my boots and my patience clean worn out. There's an alehouse called The Willing Mind, which stands on the road between Blandford and Salisbury, and it was there that night I engaged a bed. I was sitting alone in the taproom just about closing time, when the innkeeper—Allen his name was—came beside me and began yarning about the neighbours. He was a man that liked to talk and to have someone to listen to his talk, so I sat there smoking and drinking a mug of ale which he had stood me; and I took no great interest in what he said until he began to talk (as the devil would have it) about the riches of Mannering Hall.

'Meaning the large house on the right before I came to the village?' said I. 'The one that stands in its own park?'

'Exactly,' said he—and I am giving all our talk so that you may know that I am telling you the truth and hiding nothing. 'The long white house with the pillars,' said he. 'At the side of the Blandford Road.'

Now I had looked at it as I passed, and it had crossed my mind, as such thoughts will, that it was a very easy house to get into with that great row of grand windows and glass doors. I had put the thought away from me, and now here was this landlord bringing it back with his talk about the riches within. I said nothing, but I listened, and as luck would have it, he would always come back to this one subject.

'He was a miser youngman, so you can think what he is now in his age', said he. 'Well, he's had some good out of his money.'

'What good can he have had if he does not spend it?' said I.

'Well, it bought him the prettiest wife in England, and that was some good that he got out of it. She thought she would have the spending of it, but she knows the difference now.'

'Who was she then?' I asked, just for the sake of something to say.

'She was nobody at all until the old Lord made her his Lady,' said he. 'She came from up London way, and some said that she had been on the stage there, but nobody knew. The old Lord was away for a year, and when he came home he brought a young wife back with him, and there she has been ever since. Stephens, the butler, did tell me once that she was the light of the house when first she came, but what with her husband's mean and aggravatin' way, and what with her loneliness—for he hates to see a visitor within his doors; and what with his bitter words—for he has a tongue like a hornet's sting, her life all went out of her, and she became a white, silent creature, moping about the country lanes. Some say that she loved another man, and that it was just the riches of the old Lord which tempted her to be false to her lover, and that now she is eating her heart out because she has lost the one without being any nearer to the other, for she might be the poorest woman in the parish for all the money that she has the handling of.'

Well, sir, you can imagine that it did not interest me very much to hear about the quarrels between a Lord and a Lady. What did it matter to me if she hated the sound of his voice, or if he put every indignity upon her in the hope of breaking her spirit, and spoke to her as he would never have dared to speak to one of his servants? The landlord told me of these things, and of many more like them, but they passed out of my mind, for they were no concern of mine. But what I did want to hear was the form in which Lord Mannering kept his riches. Title-deeds and stock certificates are but paper, and more danger than profit to the man who takes them. But metal and stones are worth a risk. And then, as if he were answering my very thoughts, the landlord told me of Lord Mannering's great collection of gold medals, that it was the most valuable in the world, and that it was reckoned that if they were put into a sack the strongest man in the parish would not be able to raise them. Then his wife called him, and he and I went to our beds.

I am not arguing to make out a case for myself, but I beg you, sir, to bear all the facts in your mind, and to ask yourself whether a man could be more sorely tempted than I was. I make bold to say that there are few who could have held out against it. There I lay on my bed that night, a desperate man without hope or work, and with my last shilling in my pocket. I had tried to be honest, and honest folk had turned their backs upon me. They taunted me for theft; and yet they pushed me towards it. I was caught in the stream and could not get out. And then it was such a chance: the great house all lined with windows, the golden medals which could so easily be melted down. It was like putting a loaf before a starving man and expecting him not to eat it. I fought against it for a time, but it was no use. At last I sat up on the side of my bed, and I swore that that night I should either be a rich man and able to give up crime for ever, or that the irons should be on my wrists once more. Then I slipped on my clothes, and, having put a shilling on the table—for the landlord had treated me well, and I did not wish to cheat him—I passed out through the window into the garden of the inn.

There was a high wall round this garden, and I had a job to get over it, but once on the other side it was all plain sailing. I did not meet a soul upon the road, and the iron gate of the avenue was open. No one was moving at the lodge. The moon was shining, and I could see the great house glimmering white through an archway of trees. I walked up it for a quarter of a mile or so, until I was at the edge of the drive, where it ended in a broad, gravelled space before the main door. There I stood in the shadow and looked at the long building, with a full moon shining in every window and silvering the high stone front. I crouched there for some time, and I wondered where I should find the easiest entrance. The corner window of the side seemed to be the one which was least overlooked, and a screen of ivy hung heavily over it. My best chance was evidently there. I worked my way under the trees to the back of the house, and then crept along in the black shadow of the building. A dog barked and rattled his chain, but I stood waiting until he was quiet, and then I stole on once more until I came to the window which I had chosen.

It is astonishing how careless they are in the country, in places far removed from large towns, where the thought of burglars never enters their heads. I call it setting temptation in a poor man's way when he puts his hand, meaning no harm, upon a door, and finds it swing open before him. In this case it was not so bad as that, but the window was merely fastened with the ordinary catch, which I opened with a push from the blade of my knife. I pulled up the window as quickly as possible, then I thrust the knife through the slit in the shutter and prized it open. They were folding shutters, and I shoved them before me and walked into the room.

'Good evening, sir! You are very welcome!' said a voice.

I've had some starts in my life, but never one to come up to that one. There, in the opening of the shutters, within reach of my arm, was standing a woman with a small coil of wax taper burning in her hand. She was tall and straight and slender, with a beautiful white face that might have been cut out of clear marble, but her hair and eyes were as black as night. She was dressed in some sort of white dressing gown which flowed down to her feet, and what with this robe and what with her face, it seemed as if a spirit from above was standing in front of me. My knees knocked together, and I held on to the shutter with one hand to give me support. I should have turned and run away if I had had the strength, but I could only just stand and stare at her.

She soon brought me back to myself once more.

'Don't be frightened!' said she, and they were strange words for the mistress of a house to have to use to a burglar. 'I saw you out of my bedroom window when you were hiding under those trees, so I slipped downstairs, and then I heard you at the window. I should have opened it for you if you had waited, but you managed it yourself just as I came up.'

I still held in my hand the long clasp-knife with which I had opened the shutter. I was unshaven and grimed from a week on the roads. Altogether, there are few people who would have cared to face me alone at one in the morning; but this woman, if I had been her lover meeting her by appointment, could not have looked upon me with a more welcoming eye. She laid her hand upon my sleeve and drew me into the room.

'What's the meaning of this, ma'am? Don't get trying any little games upon me,' said I, in my roughest way—and I can put it on rough when I like. 'It'll be the worse for you if you play me any trick,' I added, showing her my knife.

'I will play you no trick,' said she. 'On the contrary, I am your friend, and I wish to help you.'

'Excuse me, ma'am, but I find it hard to believe that,' said I. 'Why should you wish to help me?'

'I have my own reasons,' said she; and then suddenly, with those black eyes blazing out of her white face; 'It's because I hate him, hate him, hate him! Now you understand.'

I remembered what the landlord had told me, and I did understand. I looked at her Ladyship's face, and I knew that I could trust her. She wanted to revenge herself upon her husband. She wanted to hit him where it would hurt him most—upon the pocket. She hated him so that she would even lower her pride to take such a man as me into her confidence if she could gain her end by doing so. I've hated some folk in my time, but I don't think I ever understood what hate was until I saw that woman's face in the light of the taper.

'You'll trust me now?' said she, with another coaxing touch upon my sleeve.

'Yes, Your Ladyship.'

'You know me, then?'

'I can guess who you are.'

'I dare say my wrongs are the talk of the county. But what does he care for that? He only cares for one thing in the whole world, and that you can take from him this night. Have you a bag?'

'No, Your Ladyship.'

'Shut the shutter behind you. Then no one can see the light. You are quite safe. The servants are all sleep in the other wing. I can show you where all the most valuable things are. You cannot carry them all, so we must pick the best.'

The room in which I found myself was long and low, with many rugs and skins scattered about on a polished wood floor. Small cases stood here and there, and the walls were decorated with spears and swords and paddles, and other things which find their way into museums. There were some queer clothes, too, which had been brought from savage countries, and the lady took down a large leather sack-bag from among them.

'This sleeping-sack will do,' said she. 'Now come with me and I will show you where the medals are.'

It was like a dream to me to think that this tall, white woman was the lady of the house, and that she was lending me a hand to rob her own home. I could have burst out laughing at the thought of it, and yet there was something in that pale face of hers which stopped my laughter and turned me cold and serious. She swept on in front of me like a spirit, with the green taper in her hand, and I walked behind with my sack until we came to a door at the end of this museum. It was locked, but the key was in it, and she led me through.

The room beyond was a small one, hung all round with curtains which had pictures on them. It was the hunting of a deer that was painted on it, as I remember, and in the flicker of that light you'd have sworn that the dogs and the horses were streaming round the walls. The only other thing in the room was a row of cases made of walnut, with brass ornaments. They had glass tops, and beneath this glass I saw the long lines of those gold medals, some of them as big as a plate and half an inch thick, all resting upon red velvet and glowing and gleaming in the darkness. My fingers were just itching to be at them, and I slipped my knife under the lock of one of the cases to wrench it open.

'Wait a moment,' said she, laying her hand upon my arm. 'You might do better than this.'

'I am very well satisfied, ma'am,' said I, 'and much obliged to Your Ladyship for kind assistance.'

'You can do better,' she repeated. 'Wouldn't golden sovereigns be worth more to you than these things?'

'Why,' yes,' said I. 'That's best of all.'

'Well,' said she. 'He sleeps just above our head. It is but one short staircase. There is a tin box with money enough to fill this bag under his bed.'

'How can I get it without waking him?'

'What matter if he does wake?' She looked very hard at me as she spoke. 'You could keep him from calling out.'

'No, no, ma'am, I'll have none of that.'

'Just as you like,' said she. 'I thought that you were a stout-hearted sort of man by your appearance, but I see that I made a mistake. If you are afraid to run the risk of one old man, then of course you cannot have the gold which is under his bed. You are the best judge of your own business, but I should think that you would do better at some other trade.'

'I'll not have murder on my conscience.'

'You could overpower him without harming him. I never said anything about murder. The money lies under the bed. But if you are faint-hearted, it is better that you should not attempt it.'

She worked upon me so, partly with her scorn and partly with this money that she held before my eyes, that I believe I should have yielded and taken my chances upstairs, had it not been that I saw her eyes following the struggle within me in such a crafty, malignant fashion, that it was evident she was bent upon making me the tool of her revenge, and that she would leave me no choice but to do the old man an injury or to be captured by him. She felt suddenly that she was giving herself away, and she changed her face to a kindly, friendly smile, but it was too late, for I had had my warning.

'I will not go upstairs,' said I. 'I have all I want here.'

She looked with contempt at me, and there never was a face which could look it plainer.

'Very good. You can take these medals. I should be glad if you would begin at this end. I suppose they will all be the same value when melted down, but these are the ones which are the rarest, and therefore, the most precious to him. It is not necessary to break the locks. If you press that brass knob you will find that there is a secret spring. So! Take that small one first—it is the very apple of his eye.'

She had opened one of the cases, and the beautiful things all lay exposed before me. I had my hand upon the one which she had pointed out, when suddenly a change came over her face, and she held up one finger as a warning. 'Hist!' she whispered. 'What is that?'

Far away in the silence of the house we heard a low, dragging, shuffling sound, and the distant tread of feet. She closed and fastened the case in an instant.

'It's my husband!' she whispered. 'All right. Don't be alarmed. I'll arrange it. Here! Quick, behind the tapestry!'

She pushed me behind the painted curtains upon the wall, my empty leather bag still in my hand. Then she took her taper and walked quickly into the room from which we had come. From where I stood I could see her through the open door.

'Is that you, Robert?' she cried.

The light of a candle shone through the door of the museum, and the shuffling steps came nearer. Then I saw a face in the doorway, a great, heavy face, all lines and creases, with a huge curving nose, and a pair of gold glasses fixed across it. He had to throw his head back to see through the glasses, and that great nose thrust out in front of him like the beak of some sort of fowl. He was a big man, very tall and burly, so that in his loose dressing gown his figure seemed to fill up the whole doorway. He had a pile of grey, curling hair all round his head, but his face was clean-shaven. His mouth was thin and small and prim, hidden away under his long, masterful nose. He stood there, holding the candle in front of him, and looking at his wife with a queer, malicious gleam in his eyes. It only needed that one look to tell me that he was as fond of her as she was of him.

'How's this?' he asked. 'Some new tantrum? What do you mean by wandering about the house? Why don't you go to bed?'

'I could not sleep,' she answered. She spoke languidly and wearily. If she was an actress once, she had not forgotten her calling.

'Might I suggest,' said he, in the same mocking kind of voice, 'that a good conscience is an excellent aid to sleep?'

'That cannot be true,' she answered, 'for you sleep very well.'

'I have only one thing in my life to be ashamed of,' said he, and his hair bristled up with anger until he looked like an old cockatoo. 'You know best what that is. It is a mistake which has brought its own punishment with it.'

'To me as well as to you. Remember that!'

'You have very little to whine about. It was I who stooped and you who rose.'

'Rose!'

'Yes, rose. I suppose you do not deny that it is a promotion to exchange the music hall for Mannering Hall. Fool that I was ever to take you out of your true sphere!'

'If you think so, why do you not separate?'

'Because private misery is better than public humiliation. Because it is easier to suffer for a mistake than to own to it. Because also I like to keep you in my sight, and to know that you cannot go back to him.'

'You villain! You cowardly villain!'

'Yes, yes, my lady. I know your secret ambition, but it shall never be while I live, and if it happens after my death I will at least take care that you go to him as a beggar. You and dear Edward will never have the satisfaction of squandering my savings, and you may make up your mind to that, my lady. Why are those shutters and the window open?'

'I found the night very close.'

'It is not safe. How do you know that some tramp may not be outside? Are you aware that my collection of medals is worth more than any similar collection in the world? You have left the door open also. What is there to prevent anyone from rifling the cases?

'I was here.'

'I know you were. I heard you moving about in the medal room, and that was why I came down. What were you doing?'

'Looking at the medals. What else should I be doing?'

'This curiosity is something new.' He looked suspiciously at her and moved on towards the inner room, she walking beside him.

It was at this moment that I saw something which startled me. I had laid my clasp-knife open upon the top of one of the cases, and there it lay in full view. She saw it before he did, and with a woman's cunning she held her taper out so that the light of it came between Lord Mannering's eyes and the knife. Then she took it with her left hand and held it against her gown out of his sight. He looked about from case to case—I could have put my hand at one time upon his long nose—but there was nothing to show that the medals had been tampered with, and so, still snarling and grumbling, he shuffled off into the other room once more.

And now I have to speak of what I heard rather than of what I saw, but I swear to you, as I shall stand some day before my Maker, that what I say is the truth.

When they passed into the outer room I saw him lay his candle upon the corner of one of the tables, and he sat himself down, but in such a position that he was just out of my sight. She moved behind him, as I could tell from the fact that the light of her taper threw his long, lumpy shadow upon the floor in front of him. Then he began talking about this man whom he called Edward, and every word that he said was like a blistering drop of vitriol. He spoke low, so that I could not hear it all, but from what I heard I should guess that she would as soon have been lashed with a whip. At first she said some hot words in reply, but then she was silent, and he went on and on in that cold, mocking voice of his, nagging and insulting and tormenting, until I wondered that she could bear to stand there in silence and listen to it. Then suddenly I heard him say in a sharp voice, 'Come from behind me! Let go of my collar! What! Would you dare to strike me?' There was a sound like a blow, just a soft sort of thud, and then I heard him cry out, 'My God, it's blood!' He shuffled with his feet as if he was getting up, and then I heard another blow, and he cried out, 'Oh, you she-devil!' and it was quiet, except for a dripping and splashing upon the floor.

I ran out from behind my curtain at that, and rushed into the other room, shaking all over with the horror of it. The old man had slipped down in the chair, and his dressing gown had rucked up until it looked as if he had a monstrous hump on his back. His head, with the gold glasses still fixed on his nose, was lolling over upon one side, and his little mouth was open just like a dead fish. I could not see where the blood was coming from, but I could still hear it drumming upon the floor. She stood behind him with the candle shining full upon her face. Her lips were pressed together and her eyes shining, and a touch of colour had come into each of her cheeks. Her face just wanted that to make her the most beautiful woman I had ever seen in my life.

'You've done it now!' said I.

'Yes,' said she, in her quiet way, 'I've done it now.'

'What are you going to do?' I asked. 'They'll have you for murder as sure as fate.'

'Never fear about me. I have nothing to live for, and it does not matter. Give me a hand to set him straight in the chair. It is horrible to see him like this!'

I did so, though it turned me cold all over to touch him. Some of his blood came on my hand and sickened me.

'Now,' said she, 'you may as well have the medals as anyone else. Take them and go.'

'I don't want them. I only want to get away. I was never mixed up with a business like this before.'

'Nonsense!' said she. 'You came for the medals, and here they are at your mercy. Why should you not have them? There is no one to prevent you.'

I held the bag still in my hand. She opened the case, and between us we threw a hundred or so of the medals into it. They were all from the one case, but I could not bring myself to wait for any more. Then I made for the window, for the very air of this house seemed to poison me after what I had seen and heard. As I looked back, I saw her standing there, tall and graceful, with the light in her hand just as I had seen her first. She waved goodbye, and I waved back at her and sprang out into the gravel drive.

I thank God that I can lay my hand upon my heart and say that I have never done a murder, but perhaps it would have been different if I had been able to read that woman's mind and thoughts. There might have been two bodies in the room instead of one if I could have seen behind that last smile of hers. But I thought of nothing else but of getting safely away, and it never entered my head how she might be fixing the rope round my neck. I had not taken five steps out from the window skirting down the shadow of the house in the way that I had come, when I heard a scream that might have raised the parish, and then another and another.

'Murder!' she cried. 'Murder! Murder! Help!' And her voice rang out in the quiet of the night-time and sounded over the whole countryside. It went through my head, that dreadful cry. In an instant lights began to move and windows to fly up, not only in the house behind me, but at the lodge and in the stables in front. Like a frightened rabbit I bolted down the drive, but I heard the clang of the gate being shut before I could reach it. Then I hid my bag of medals under some dry fagots, and I tried to get away across the park, but someone saw me in the moonlight, and presently I had half a dozen of them with dogs upon my heels. I crouched down among the brambles, but those dogs were too many for me, and I was glad enough when the men came up and prevented me from being torn into pieces. They seized me, and dragged me back to the room from which I had come.

'Is this the man, Your Ladyship?' asked the oldest of them—the same whom I found out afterwards to be the butler.

She had been bending over the body, with her handkerchief to her eyes, and now she turned upon me with the face of a fury. Oh, what an actress that woman was!

'Yes, yes, it is the very man,' she cried. 'Oh, you villain, you cruel villain, to treat an old man so!'

There was a man there who seemed to be a village constable. He laid his hand upon my shoulder.

'What do you say to that?' said he.

'It was she who did it,' I cried, pointing at the woman, whose eyes never flinched before mine.

'Come! Come! Try another!' said the constable, and one of the menservants struck at me with his fist.

'I tell you that I saw her do it. She stabbed him twice with a knife. She first helped me to rob him, and then she murdered him.'

The footman tried to strike me again, but she held up her hand.

'Do not hurt him,' said she. 'I think that his punishment may safely be left to the law.'

'I'll see to that, Your Ladyship,' said the constable. 'Your Ladyship actually saw the crime committed, did you not?'

'Yes, yes, I saw it with my own eyes. It was horrible. We heard the noise and we came down. My poor husband was in front. The man had one of the cases open, and was filling a black leather bag which he held in his hand. He rushed past us, and my husband seized him. There was a struggle, and he stabbed him twice. There you can see the blood upon his hands. If I am not mistaken, his knife is still in Lord Mannering's body.'

'Look at the blood upon her hands!' I cried.

'She has been holding up his Lordship's head, you lying

rascal,' said the butler.

'And here's the very sack her Ladyship spoke of,' said the constable, as a groom came in with the one which I had dropped in my flight. 'And here are the medals inside it. That's good enough for me. We will keep him safe here tonight, and tomorrow the inspector and I can take him into Salisbury.'

'Poor creature,' said the woman. 'For my own part, I forgive him of any injury which he has done me. Who knows what temptation may have driven him to crime? His conscience and the law will give him punishment enough without any reproach of mine rendering it more bitter.'

I could not answer—I tell you, sir, I could not answer, so taken aback was I by the assurance of the woman. And so, seeming by my silence to agree to all that she had said, I was dragged away by the butler and the constable into the cellar, in which they locked me for the night.

There, sir, I have told you the whole story of the events which led up to the murder of Lord Mannering by his wife upon the night of 14 September 1894. Perhaps you will put my statement on one side as the constable did at Mannering Towers, or the judge afterwards at the county assizes. Or perhaps you will see that there is a ring of truth in what I say, and you will follow it up, and so make your name forever as a man who does not grudge personal trouble where justice is to be done. I have only you to look to, sir, and if you will clear my name of this false accusation, then I will worship you as one man never yet worshipped another. But if you fail me, then I give you my solemn promise that I will rope myself up, this day and month, to the bar of my window, and from that time on I will come to plague you in your dreams if ever yet one man was able to come back to haunt another. What I ask you to do is very simple. Make inquiries about this woman, watch her, learn her past history, find out what she is making of the money which has come to her, and whether there is not a man Edward as I have stated. If from all this you learn anything which shows you her real character, or which seems to you to corroborate to the story which I have told you, then I am sure that I can rely upon your goodness of heart to come to the rescue of an innocent man.

THE TELL-TALE HEART

Edgar Allan Poe

True! Nervous—very, very dreadfully nervous I had been and am! But why will you say that I am mad? The disease had sharpened my senses—not destroyed—not dulled them. Above all was the sense of hearing acute. I heard all things in the heaven and in the earth. I heard many things in hell. How, then, am I mad? Hearken! And observe how healthily—how calmly I can tell you the whole story.

It is impossible to tell how first the idea entered my brain; but once conceived, it haunted me day and night. Object there was none. Passion there was none. I loved the old man. He had never wronged me. He had never given me insult. For his gold I had no desire. I think it was his eye! Yes, it was this! One of his eyes resembled that of a vulture—a pale blue eye, with a film over it. Whenever it fell upon me, my blood ran cold; and so by degrees—very gradually—I made up my mind to take the life of the old man, and thus rid myself of the eye forever.

Now this is the point. You fancy me mad. Madmen know nothing. But you should have seen me. You should have seen how wisely I proceeded—with what caution—with what foresight—with what dissimulation I went to work!

I was never kinder to the old man than during the whole week before I killed him. And every night, about midnight, I turned the latch of his door and opened it—oh, so gently! And then, when I had made an opening sufficient for my head, I put in a dark lantern, all closed, closed, so that no light shone out, and then I thrust in my head. Oh, you would have laughed to see how cunningly I thrust it in! I moved it slowly—very, very slowly, so that I might not disturb the old man's sleep. It took me an hour to place my whole head within the opening so far that I could see him as he lay upon his bed. Ha!—Would a madman have been so wise as this? And then, when my head was well in the room, I undid the lantern cautiously—oh, so cautiously—cautiously (for the hinges creaked)—I undid it just so much that a single thin ray fell upon the vulture eye. And this I did for seven long nights—every night just at midnight—but I found the eye always closed; and so it was impossible to do the work; for it was not the old man who vexed me, but his Evil Eye. And every morning, when the day broke, I went boldly into his chamber, and spoke courageously to him, calling him by name in a hearty tone, and inquiring how he had passed the night. So you see he would have been a very profound old man, indeed, to suspect that every night, just at twelve, I looked in upon him while he slept.

Upon the eighth night I was more than usually cautious in opening the door. A watch's minute hand moves more quickly than did mine. Never before that night had I felt the extent of my own powers—of my sagacity. I could scarcely contain my feelings of triumph. To think that there I was, opening the door, little by little, and he did not even dream of my secret deeds or thoughts. I fairly chuckled at the idea; and perhaps he heard me; for he moved on the bed suddenly, as if startled.

Now you may think that I drew back—but no. His room was as black as pitch with the thick darkness (for the shutters were close fastened, through fear of robbers), and so I knew that he could not see the opening of the door, and I kept pushing it on steadily, steadily.

I had my head in, and was about to open the lantern, when my thumb slipped upon the tin fastening, and the old man sprang up in bed, crying out: 'Who's there?'

I kept quite still and said nothing. For a whole hour I did not move a muscle, and in the meantime I did not hear him lie down. He was still sitting up in the bed listening—just as I have done, night after night, hearkening to the death watches in the wall.

Presently I heard a slight groan, and I knew it was the groan of mortal terror. It was not a groan of pain or grief—oh no! It was the low stifled sound that arises from the bottom of the soul when overcharged with awe. I knew the sound well. Many a night, just at midnight, when all the world slept, it has welled up from my own bosom, deepening, with its dreadful echo, the terrors that distracted me. I say I knew it well. I knew what the old man felt, and pitied him, although I chuckled at heart. I knew that he had been lying awake ever since the first slight noise, when he had turned in the bed. His fears had been ever since growing upon him. He had been trying to fancy them causeless, but could not. He had been saying to himself: 'It is nothing but the wind in the chimney—it is only a mouse crossing the floor,' or 'It is merely a cricket which has made a single chirp.' Yes, he had been trying to comfort himself with these suppositions; but he had found all in vain. All in vain; because death, in approaching him, had stalked with his black shadow before him, and enveloped the victim. And it was the mournful influence of the unperceived shadow that caused him to feel—although he neither saw nor heard—to feel the presence of my head within the room.

When I had waited a long time, very patiently, without hearing him lie down, I resolved to open a little—a very, very little crevice in the lantern. So I opened it—you cannot imagine how stealthily, stealthily—until, at length, a single dim ray, like the thread of the spider, shot out from the crevice and fell upon the vulture eye.

It was open—wide, wide open—and I grew furious as I gazed upon it. I saw it with perfect distinctness—all a dull blue, with a hideous veil over it that chilled the very marrow in my bones; but I could see nothing else of the old man's face or person: for I had directed the ray, as if by instinct, precisely upon the damned spot.

And now—have I not told you that what you mistake for madness is but over-acuteness of the senses?—now, I say, there came to my ears a low, dull, quick sound, such as a watch makes when enveloped in cotton. I knew that sound well too. It was the beating of the old man's heart. It increased my fury, as the beating of a drum stimulates the soldier into courage.

But even yet I refrained and kept still. I scarcely breathed. I held the lantern motionless. I tried how steadily I could maintain the ray upon the eye. Meantime the hellish tattoo of the heart increased. It grew quicker and quicker and louder and louder every instant. The old man's terror must have been extreme! It grew louder, I say, louder every moment!—Do you mark me well? I have told you that I am nervous: so I am. And now at the dead hour of night, amid the dreadful silence of that old house, so strange a noise as this excited me to uncontrollable terror. Yet, for some minutes longer I refrained and stood still.

But the beating grew louder, louder! I thought the heart must burst. And now a new anxiety seized me—the sound would be heard by a neighbour! The old man's hour had come! With a loud yell, I threw open the lantern and leaped into the room. He shrieked once—once only. In an instant I dragged him to the floor, and pulled the heavy bed over him. I then smiled gaily, to find the deed so far done. But, for many minutes, the heart beat on with a muffled sound. This, however, did not vex me; it would not be heard through the wall. At length it ceased. The old man was dead. I removed the bed and examined the corpse. Yes, he was stone, stone dead. I placed my hand upon the heart and held it there many minutes. There was no pulsation. He was stone dead. His eye would trouble me no more.

If still you think me mad, you will think so no longer when I describe the wise precautions I took for the concealment of the body. The night waned, and I worked hastily, but in silence. First of all I dismembered the corpse. I cut off the head and the arms and the legs.

I then took up three planks from the flooring of the chamber, and deposited all between the scantlings. I then replaced the boards so cleverly, so cunningly, that no human eye—not even his—could have detected anything wrong. There was nothing to wash out—no stain of any kind—no blood-spot whatever. I had been too wary for that. A tub had caught all—Ha! Ha!

When I had made an end of these labours, it was four o'clock—still dark as midnight. As the bell sounded the hour, there came a knocking at the street door. I went down to open it with a light heart—for what had I now to fear? There entered three men, who introduced themselves, with perfect suavity, as officers of the police. A shriek had been heard by a neighbour during the night: suspicion of foul play had been aroused; information had been lodged at the police office, and they (the officers) had been deputed to search the premises.

I smiled—for what had I to fear? I bade the gentlemen welcome. The shriek, I said, was my own in a dream. The old man, I mentioned, was absent in the country. I took my visitors all over the house. I bade them search—search well. I led them, at length, to his chamber. I showed them his treasures, secure, undisturbed. In the enthusiasm of my confidence, I brought chairs into the room, and desired them here to rest from their fatigues, while I myself, in the wild audacity of my perfect triumph, placed my own seat upon the very spot beneath which reposed the corpse of the victim.

The officers were satisfied. My manner had convinced them. I was singularly at ease. They sat, and while I answered cheerily, they chatted familiar things. But, ere long, I felt myself getting pale and wished them gone. My head ached, and I fancied a ringing in my ears: but still they sat and still chatted. The ringing became more distinct—it continued and became more distinct: I talked more freely to get rid of the feeling: but it continued and gained definiteness—until, at length, I found that the noise was not within my ears.

No doubt I now grew very pale—but I talked more fluently, and with a heightened voice. Yet the sound increased—and what could I do? It was a low, dull, quick sound—much such a sound as a watch makes when enveloped in cotton. I gasped for breath—and yet the officers heard it not. I talked more quickly—more vehemently; but the noise steadily increased. Why would they not be gone? I paced the floor to and fro with heavy strides, as if excited to fury by the observation of the men—but the noise steadily increased. Oh, God; what could I do? I foamed—I raved—I swore! I swung the chair upon which I had been sitting, and grated it upon the boards, but the noise arose over all and continually increased. It grew louder—louder—louder! And still the men chatted pleasantly, and smiled. Was it possible they heard not? Almighty God!—No, no! They heard!—They suspected—They knew!—They were making a mockery of my horror!—This I thought, and this I think. But anything was better than this agony! Anything was more tolerable than this derision! I could bear those hypocritical smiles no longer! I felt that I must scream or die!—And now—Again!—Hark! Louder! louder! Louder!

'Villains!' I shrieked, 'Dissemble no more! I admit the deed!—Tear up the planks!—Here, here!—It is the beating of his hideous heart!'

THE MAGIC SHOP

H.G. Wells

I had seen the Magic Shop from afar several times; I had passed it once or twice, a shop window of alluring little objects, magic balls, magic hens, wonderful cones, ventriloquist dolls, the material of the basket trick, packs of cards that *looked* all right, and all that sort of thing, but never had I thought of going in until one day, almost without warning, Gip hauled me by my finger right up to the window, and so conducted himself that there was nothing for it but to take him in. I had not thought the place was there, to tell the truth—a modest-sized frontage in Regent Street, between the picture shop and the place where the chicks run about just out of patent incubators, but there it was sure enough. I had fancied it was down near the Circus, or round the corner in Oxford Street, or even in Holborn; always over the way and a little inaccessible it had been, with something of the mirage in its position; but here it was now quite indisputably, and the fat end of Gip's pointing finger made a noise upon the glass.

'If I was rich,' said Gip, dabbing a finger at the Disappearing Egg, 'I'd buy myself that. And that'—which was The Crying Baby, Very Human—'and that,' which was a mystery, and called, so a neat card asserted, 'Buy One and Astonish Your Friends.'

'Anything,' said Gip, 'will disappear under one of those cones. I have read about it in a book.'

'And there, dadda, is the Vanishing Halfpenny—only they've put it this way up so's we can't see how it's done.'

Gip, dear boy, inherits his mother's breeding, and he did not propose to enter the shop or worry in any way; only, you know, quite unconsciously he lugged my finger doorward, and he made his interest clear.

'That,' he said, and pointed to the Magic Bottle.

'If you had that?' I said; at which promising inquiry he looked up with a sudden radiance.

'I could show it to Jessie,' he said, thoughtful as ever of others.

'It's less than a hundred days to your birthday, Gibbles,' I said, and laid my hand on the door-handle.

Gip made no answer, but his grip tightened on my finger, and so we came into the shop.

It was no common shop this; it was a magic shop, and all the prancing precedence Gip would have taken in the matter of mere toys was wanting. He left the burden of the conversation to me.

It was a little, narrow shop, not very well lit, and the door-bell pinged again with a plaintive note as we closed it behind us. For a moment or so we were alone and could glance about us. There was a tiger in papier-mache on the glass case that covered the low counter—a grave, kind-eyed tiger that waggled his head in a methodical manner; there were several crystal spheres, a china hand holding magic cards, a stock of magic fish bowls in various sizes, and an immodest magic hat that shamelessly displayed its springs. On the floor were magic mirrors; one to draw you out long and thin, one to swell your head and vanish your legs, and one to make you short and fat like a draught; and while we were laughing at these the shopman, as I suppose, came in.

At any rate, there he was behind the counter—a curious, sallow, dark man, with one ear larger than the other and a chin like the toe-cap of a boot.

'What can we have the pleasure?' he said, spreading his long, magic fingers on the glass case; and so with a start we were aware of him.

'I want,' I said, 'to buy my little boy a few simple tricks.'

'Legerdemain?' he asked. 'Mechanical? Domestic?'

'Anything amusing?' said I.

'Um!' said the shopman, and scratched his head for a moment as if thinking. Then, quite distinctly, he drew from his head a glass ball. 'Something in this way?' he said, and held it out.

The action was unexpected. I had seen the trick done at entertainments endless times before—it's part of the common stock of conjurers—but I had not expected it here.

'That's good,' I said, with a laugh.

'Isn't it?' said the shopman.

Gip stretched out his disengaged hand to take this object and found merely a blank palm.

'It's in your pocket,' said the shopman, and there it was!

'How much will that be?' I asked.

'We make no charge for glass balls,' said the shopman politely. 'We get them,'—he picked one out of his elbow as he spoke—'free.' He produced another from the back of his neck, and laid it beside its predecessor on the counter. Gip regarded his glass ball sagely, then directed a look of inquiry at the two on the counter, and finally brought his round-eyed scrutiny to the shopman, who smiled.

'You may have those too,' said the shopman, 'and, if you *don't* mind, one from my mouth. *So!*'

Gip counselled me mutely for a moment, and then in a profound silence put away the four balls, resumed my reassuring finger, and nerved himself for the next event.

'We get all our smaller tricks in that way,' the shopman remarked.

I laughed in the manner of one who subscribes to a jest. 'Instead of going to the wholesale shop,' I said. 'Of course, it's cheaper.'

'In a way,' the shopman said. 'Though we pay in the end. But not so heavily—as people suppose... Our larger tricks, and our daily provisions and all the other things we want, we get out of that hat... And you know, sir, if you'll excuse my saying it, there *isn't* a wholesale shop, not for Genuine Magic goods, sir. I don't know if you noticed our inscription—the Genuine Magic Shop.' He drew a business card from his cheek and handed it to me. 'Genuine,' he said, with his finger on the word, and added, 'There is absolutely no deception, sir.'

He seemed to be carrying out the joke pretty thoroughly, I thought.

He turned to Gip with a smile of remarkable affability. 'You, you know, are the Right Sort of Boy.'

I was surprised at his knowing that, because, in the interests of discipline, we keep it rather a secret even at home; but Gip received it in unflinching silence, keeping a steadfast eye on him.

'It's only the Right Sort of Boy that gets through that doorway.'

And, as if by way of illustration, there came a rattling at

the door, and a squeaking little voice could be faintly heard. 'Nyar! I *warn* 'a go in there, dadda, I *warn* 'a go in there. Ny-a-a-ah!' And then the accents of a down-trodden parent, urging consolations and propitiations. 'It's locked, Edward,' he said.

'But it isn't,' said I.

'It is, sir,' said the shopman, 'always—for that sort of child,' and as he spoke we had a glimpse of the other youngster, a little, white face, pallid from sweet-eating and over-sapid food, and distorted by evil passions, a ruthless little egotist, pawing at the enchanted pane. 'It's no good, sir,' said the shopman, as I moved, with my natural helpfulness, doorward, and presently the spoilt child was carried off howling.

'How do you manage that?' I said, breathing a little more freely.

'Magic!' said the shopman, with a careless wave of the hand, and behold! Sparks of coloured fire flew out of his fingers and vanished into the shadows of the shop.

'You were saying,' he said, addressing himself to Gip, 'before you came in, that you would like one of our 'Buy One and Astonish your Friends' boxes?'

Gip, after a gallant effort, said 'Yes.'

'It's in your pocket.'

And leaning over the counter—he really had an extraordinarily long body—this amazing person produced the article in the customary conjurer's manner. 'Paper,' he said, and took a sheet out of the empty hat with the springs; 'string,' and behold his mouth was a string-box, from which he drew an unending thread, which when he had tied his parcel he bit off—and, it seemed to me, swallowed the ball of string. And then he lit a candle at the nose of one of the ventriloquist's dummies, stuck one of his fingers (which had become sealing-wax red) into the flame, and so sealed the parcel. 'Then there was the Disappearing Egg,' he remarked, and produced one from within my coat-breast and packed it, and also The Crying Baby, Very Human. I handed each parcel to Gip as it was ready, and he clasped them to his chest.

He said very little, but his eyes were eloquent; the clutch of his arms was eloquent. He was the playground of unspeakable emotions. These, you know, were *real* Magics. Then, with a start, I discovered something moving about in my hat—something soft and jumpy. I whipped it off, and a ruffled pigeon—no doubt a confederate—dropped out and ran on the counter, and went, I fancy, into a cardboard box behind the papier-mache tiger.

'Tut, tut!' said the shopman, dexterously relieving me of my headdress; 'careless bird, and—as I live—nesting!'

He shook my hat, and shook out into his extended hand two or three eggs, a large marble, a watch, about half-a-dozen of the inevitable glass balls, and then crumpled, crinkled paper, more and more and more, talking all the time of the way in which people neglect to brush their hats *inside* as well as out, politely, of course, but with a certain personal application. 'All sorts of things accumulate, sir... Not *you*, of course, in particular... Nearly every customer... Astonishing what they carry about with them...' The crumpled paper rose and billowed on the counter more and more and more, until he was nearly hidden from us, until he was altogether hidden, and still his voice went on and on. 'We none of us know what the fair semblance of a human being may conceal, sir. Are we all then no better than brushed exteriors, whited sepulchres—'

His voice stopped—exactly like when you hit a neighbour's gramophone with a well-aimed brick, the same instant silence, and the rustle of the paper stopped, and everything was still...

'Have you done with my hat?' I said, after an interval.

There was no answer.

I stared at Gip, and Gip stared at me, and there were our distortions in the magic mirrors, looking very rum, and grave, and quiet...

'I think we'll go now,' I said. 'Will you tell me how much all this comes to?...

'I say,' I said, on a rather louder note, 'I want the bill; and my hat, please.'

It might have been a sniff from behind the paper pile...

'Let's look behind the counter, Gip,' I said. 'He's making fun of us.'

I led Gip round the head-wagging tiger, and what do you think there was behind the counter? No one at all! Only my hat on the floor, and a common conjurer's lop-eared white rabbit lost in meditation, and looking as stupid and crumpled as only a conjurer's rabbit can do. I resumed my hat, and the rabbit lolloped a lollop or so out of my way.

'Dadda!' said Gip, in a guilty whisper.

'What is it, Gip?' said I.

'I *do* like this shop, dadda.'

'So should I,' I said to myself, 'if the counter wouldn't suddenly extend itself to shut one off from the door.' But I didn't call Gip's attention to that. 'Pussy!' he said, with a hand out to the rabbit as it came lolloping past us; 'Pussy, do Gip a magic!' And his eyes followed it as it squeezed through a door I had certainly not remarked a moment before. Then this door opened wider, and the man with one ear larger than the other appeared again. He was smiling still, but his eye met mine with something between amusement and defiance. 'You'd like to see our showroom, sir,' he said, with an innocent suavity.

Gip tugged my finger forward. I glanced at the counter and met the shopman's eye again. I was beginning to think the magic just a little too genuine. 'We haven't VERY much time,' I said. But somehow we were inside the showroom before I could finish that.

'All goods of the same quality,' said the shopman, rubbing his flexible hands together, 'and that is the Best. Nothing in the place that isn't genuine Magic, and warranted thoroughly rum. Excuse me, sir!'

I felt him pull at something that clung to my coat-sleeve, and then I saw he held a little, wriggling red demon by the tail—the little creature bit and fought and tried to get at his hand—and in a moment he tossed it carelessly behind a counter. No doubt the thing was only an image of twisted indiarubber, but for the moment—! And his gesture was exactly that of a man who handles some petty biting bit of vermin. I glanced at Gip, but Gip was looking at a magic rocking-horse. I was glad he hadn't seen the thing. 'I say,' I said, in an undertone, and indicating Gip and the red demon with my eyes, 'you haven't many things like *that* about, have you?'

'None of ours! Probably brought it with you,' said the shopman—also in an undertone, and with a more dazzling smile than ever. 'Astonishing what people will carry about with them unawares!' And then to Gip, 'Do you see anything you fancy here?'

There were many things that Gip fancied there.

He turned to this astonishing tradesman with mingled confidence and respect. 'Is that a Magic Sword?' he said.

'A Magic Toy Sword. It neither bends, breaks, nor cuts the fingers. It renders the bearer invincible in battle against anyone under eighteen. Half-a-crown to seven and sixpence, according to size. These panoplies on cards are for juvenile knights-errant and very useful—shield of safety, sandals of swiftness, helmet of invisibility.'

'Oh, daddy!' gasped Gip.

I tried to find out what they cost, but the shopman did not heed me. He had got Gip now; he had got him away from my finger; he had embarked upon the exposition of all his confounded stock, and nothing was going to stop him. Presently I saw with a qualm of distrust and something very like jealousy that Gip had hold of this person's finger as usually he has hold of mine. No doubt the fellow was interesting, I thought, and had an interestingly faked lot of stuff, really *good* faked stuff, still—

I wandered after them, saying very little, but keeping an eye on this prestidigital fellow. After all, Gip was enjoying it. And no doubt when the time came to go we should be able to go quite easily.

It was a long, rambling place, that showroom, a gallery broken up by stands and stalls and pillars, with archways leading off to other departments, in which the queerest-looking assistants loafed and stared at one, and with perplexing mirrors and curtains. So perplexing, indeed, were these that I was presently unable to make out the door by which we had come.

The shopman showed Gip magic trains that ran without steam or clockwork, just as you set the signals, and then some very, very valuable boxes of soldiers that all came alive directly as you took off the lid and said—I myself haven't a very quick ear and it was a tongue-twisting sound, but Gip—he has his mother's ear—got it in no time. 'Bravo!' said the shopman, putting the men back into the box unceremoniously and handing it to Gip. 'Now,' said the shopman, and in a moment Gip had made them all alive again.

'You'll take that box?' asked the shopman.

'We'll take that box,' said I, 'unless you charge its full value. In which case it would need a Trust Magnate—'

'Dear heart! *No!*' and the shopman swept the little men back again, shut the lid, waved the box in the air, and there it was, in brown paper, tied up and—*with Gip's full name and address on the paper*!

The shopman laughed at my amazement.

'This is the genuine magic,' he said. 'The real thing.'

'It's a little too genuine for my taste,' I said again.

After that he fell to showing Gip tricks, odd tricks, and still odder the way they were done. He explained them, he turned them inside out, and there was the dear little chap nodding his busy bit of a head in the sagest manner.

I did not attend as well as I might. 'Hey, presto!' said the Magic Shopman, and then would come the clear, small 'Hey, presto!' of the boy. But I was distracted by other things. It was being borne in upon me just how tremendously rum this place was; it was, so to speak, inundated by a sense of rumness. There was something a little rum about the fixtures even, about the ceiling, about the floor, about the casually distributed chairs. I had a queer feeling that whenever I wasn't looking at them straight they went askew, and moved about, and played a noiseless puss-in-the-corner behind my back. And the cornice had a serpentine design with masks—masks altogether too expressive for proper plaster.

Then abruptly my attention was caught by one of the odd-looking assistants. He was some way off and evidently unaware of my presence—I saw a sort of three-quarter length of him over a pile of toys and through an arch—and, you know, he was leaning against a pillar in an idle sort of way doing the most horrid things with his features! The particular horrid thing he did was with his nose. He did it just as though he was idle and wanted to amuse himself. First of all it was a short, blobby nose, and then suddenly he shot it out like a telescope, and then out it flew and became thinner and thinner until it was like a long, red, flexible whip. Like a thing in a nightmare it was! He flourished it about and flung it forth as a fly-fisher flings his line.

My instant thought was that Gip mustn't see him. I turned about, and there was Gip quite preoccupied with the shopman, and thinking no evil. They were whispering together and looking at me. Gip was standing on a little stool, and the shopman was holding a sort of big drum in his hand.

'Hide and seek, dadda!' cried Gip. 'You're He!'

And before I could do anything to prevent it, the shopman had clapped the big drum over him. I saw what was up directly. 'Take that off,' I cried, 'this instant! You'll frighten the boy. Take it off!'

The shopman with the unequal ears did so without a word, and held the big cylinder towards me to show its emptiness. And the little stool was vacant! In that instant my boy had utterly disappeared...

You know, perhaps, that sinister something that comes like a hand out of the unseen and grips your heart about. You know it takes your common self away and leaves you tense and deliberate, neither slow nor hasty, neither angry nor afraid. So it was with me.

I came up to this grinning shopman and kicked his stool aside.

'Stop this folly!' I said. 'Where is my boy?'

'You see,' he said, still displaying the drum's interior, 'there is no deception——'

I put out my hand to grip him, and he eluded me by a dexterous movement. I snatched again, and he turned from me and pushed open a door to escape. 'Stop!' I said, and he laughed, receding. I leapt after him—into utter darkness.

THUD!

'Lor' bless my 'eart! I didn't see you coming, sir!'

I was in Regent Street, and I had collided with a decent-looking working man; and a yard away, perhaps, and looking a little perplexed with himself, was Gip. There was some sort of apology, and then Gip had turned and come to me with a bright little smile, as though for a moment he had missed me.

And he was carrying four parcels in his arm!

He secured immediate possession of my finger.

For the second I was rather at a loss. I stared round to see the door of the magic shop, and, behold, it was not there! There was no door, no shop, nothing, only the common pilaster between the shop where they sell pictures and the window with the chicks!

I did the only thing possible in that mental tumult; I walked straight to the kerbstone and held up my umbrella for a cab.

'Ansoms,' said Gip, in a note of culminating exultation.

I helped him in, recalled my address with an effort, and got in also. Something unusual proclaimed itself in my tailcoat pocket, and I felt and discovered a glass ball. With a petulant expression I flung it into the street.

Gip said nothing.

For a space neither of us spoke.

'Dadda!' said Gip, at last, 'that *was* a proper shop!'

I came round with that to the problem of just how the whole thing had seemed to him. He looked completely undamaged—so far, good; he was neither scared nor unhinged, he was simply tremendously satisfied with the afternoon's entertainment, and there in his arms were the four parcels.

Confound it! What could be in them?

'Um!' I said. 'Little boys can't go to shops like that every day.'

He received this with his usual stoicism, and for a moment I was sorry I was his father and not his mother, and so couldn't suddenly there, coram publico, in our hansom, kiss him. After all, I thought, the thing wasn't so very bad.

But it was only when we opened the parcels that I really began to be reassured. Three of them contained boxes of soldiers, quite ordinary lead soldiers, but of so good a quality as to make Gip altogether forget that originally these parcels had been Magic Tricks of the only genuine sort, and the fourth contained a kitten, a little living white kitten, in excellent health and appetite and temper.

I saw this unpacking with a sort of provisional relief. I hung about in the nursery for quite an unconscionable time...

That happened six months ago. And now I am beginning to believe it is all right. The kitten had only the magic natural to all kittens, and the soldiers seem as steady a company as any colonel could desire. And Gip—?

The intelligent parent will understand that I have to go cautiously with Gip.

But I went so far as this one day. I said, 'How would you like your soldiers to come alive, Gip, and march about by themselves?'

'Mine do,' said Gip. 'I just have to say a word I know before I open the lid.'

'Then they march about alone?'

'Oh, *quite*, dadda. I shouldn't like them if they didn't do that.'

I displayed no unbecoming surprise, and since then I have

taken occasion to drop in upon him once or twice, unannounced, when the soldiers were about, but so far I have never discovered them performing in anything like a magical manner.

It's so difficult to tell.

There's also a question of finance. I have an incurable habit of paying bills. I have been up and down Regent Street several times, looking for that shop. I am inclined to think, indeed, that in that matter honour is satisfied, and that, since Gip's name and address are known to them, I may very well leave it to these people, whoever they may be, to send in their bill in their own time.

THE SIGNAL-MAN

Charles Dickens

'Halloa! Below there!'

When he heard a voice thus calling to him, he was standing at the door of his box, with a flag in his hand, furled round its short pole. One would have thought, considering the nature of the ground, that he could not have doubted from what quarter the voice came; but instead of looking up to where I stood on the top of the steep cutting nearly over his head, he turned himself about, and looked down the Line. There was something remarkable in his manner of doing so, though I could not have said for my life what. But I know it was remarkable enough to attract my notice, even though his figure was foreshortened and shadowed, down in the deep trench, and mine was high above him, so steeped in the glow of an angry sunset, that I had shaded my eyes with my hand before I saw him at all.

'Halloa! Below!'

From looking down the Line, he turned himself about again, and, raising his eyes, saw my figure high above him.

'Is there any path by which I can come down and speak to you?'

He looked up at me without replying, and I looked down at him without pressing him too soon with a repetition of my idle question. Just then there came a vague vibration in the earth and air, quickly changing into a violent pulsation, and an oncoming rush that caused me to start back, as though it had force to draw me down. When such vapour as rose to my height from this rapid train had passed me, and was skimming away over the landscape, I looked down again, and saw him refurling the flag he had shown while the train went by.

I repeated my inquiry. After a pause, during which he seemed to regard me with fixed attention, he motioned with his rolled-up flag towards a point on my level, some two or three hundred yards distant. I called down to him, 'All right!' and made for that point. There, by dint of looking closely about me, I found a rough zigzag descending path notched out, which I followed.

The cutting was extremely deep, and unusually precipitate. It was made through a clammy stone, that became oozier and wetter as I went down. For these reasons, I found the way long enough to give me time to recall a singular air of reluctance or compulsion with which he had pointed out the path.

When I came down low enough upon the zigzag descent to see him again, I saw that he was standing between the rails on the way by which the train had lately passed, in an attitude as if he were waiting for me to appear. He had his left hand at his chin, and that left elbow rested on his right hand, crossed over his breast. His attitude was one of such expectation and watchfulness that I stopped a moment, wondering at it.

I resumed my downward way, and stepping out upon the level of the railroad, and drawing nearer to him, saw that he was a dark sallow man, with a dark beard and rather heavy eyebrows. His post was in as solitary and dismal a place as ever I saw. On either side, a dripping-wet wall of jagged stone, excluding all view but a strip of sky; the perspective one way only a crooked prolongation of this great dungeon; the shorter perspective in the other direction terminating in a gloomy red light, and the gloomier entrance to a black tunnel, in whose massive architecture there was a barbarous, depressing, and forbidding air. So little sunlight ever found its way to this spot, that it had an earthy, deadly smell; and so much cold wind rushed through it, that it struck chill to me, as if I had left the natural world.

Before he stirred, I was near enough to him to have touched him. Not even then removing his eyes from mine, he stepped back one step, and lifted his hand.

This was a lonesome post to occupy (I said), and it had riveted my attention when I looked down from up yonder. A visitor was a rarity, I should suppose; not an unwelcome rarity, I hoped? In me, he merely saw a man who had been shut up within narrow limits all his life, and who, being at last set free, had a newly-awakened interest in these great works. To such purpose I spoke to him; but I am far from sure of the terms I used; for, besides that I am not happy in opening any conversation, there was something in the man that daunted me.

He directed a most curious look towards the red light near the tunnel's mouth, and looked all about it, as if something were missing from it, and then looked it me.

That light was part of his charge? Was it not?

He answered in a low voice—'Don't you know it is?'

The monstrous thought came into my mind, as I perused the fixed eyes and the saturnine face, that this was a spirit, not a man. I have speculated since, whether there may have been infection in his mind.

In my turn, I stepped back. But in making the action, I detected in his eyes some latent fear of me. This put the monstrous thought to flight.

'You look at me,' I said, forcing a smile, 'as if you had a dread of me.'

'I was doubtful,' he returned, 'whether I had seen you before.'

'Where?'

He pointed to the red light he had looked at.

'There?' I said.

Intently watchful of me, he replied (but without sound), 'Yes.'

'My good fellow, what should I do there? However, be that as it may, I never was there, you may swear.'

'I think I may,' he rejoined. 'Yes; I am sure I may.'

His manner cleared, like my own. He replied to my remarks with readiness, and in well-chosen words. Had he much to do there? Yes; that was to say, he had enough responsibility to bear; but exactness and watchfulness were what was required of him, and of actual work—manual labour—he had next to none. To change that signal, to trim those lights, and to turn this iron handle now and then, was all he had to do under that head. Regarding those many long and lonely hours of which I seemed to make so much, he could only say that the routine of his life had shaped itself into that form, and he had grown used to it. He had taught himself a language down here—if only to know it by sight, and to have formed his own crude ideas of its pronunciation, could be called learning it. He had also worked at fractions and decimals, and tried a little algebra; but he was, and had been as a boy, a poor hand at figures. Was it necessary for him when on duty always to remain in that channel of damp air, and could he never rise into the sunshine from between those high stone walls? Why, that depended upon times and circumstances. Under some conditions there would be less upon the Line than under others, and the same held good as to certain hours of the day and night. In bright weather, he did choose occasions for getting a little above these lower shadows; but, being at all times liable to be called by his electric bell, and at such times listening for it with redoubled anxiety, the relief was less than I would suppose.

He took me into his box, where there was a fire, a desk for an official book in which he had to make certain entries, a telegraphic instrument with its dial, face, and needles, and the little bell of which he had spoken. On my trusting that he would excuse the remark that he had been well educated, and (I hoped I might say without offence) perhaps educated above that station, he observed that instances of slight incongruity in such wise would rarely be found wanting among large bodies of men; that he had heard it was so in workhouses, in the police force, even in that last desperate resource, the army; and that he knew it was so, more or less, in any great railway staff. He had been, when young (if I could believe it, sitting in that hut—he scarcely could), a student of natural philosophy, and had attended lectures; but he had run wild, misused his opportunities, gone down, and never risen again. He had no complaint to offer about that. He had made his bed, and he lay upon it. It was far too late to make another.

All that I have here condensed he said in a quiet manner, with his grave dark regards divided between me and the fire. He threw in the word, 'Sir,' from time to time, and especially when he referred to his youth—as though to request me to understand that he claimed to be nothing but what I found him. He was several times interrupted by the little bell, and had to read off messages, and send replies. Once he had to stand without the door, and display a flag as a train passed, and make some verbal communication to the driver. In the discharge of his duties, I observed him to be remarkably exact and vigilant, breaking off his discourse at a syllable, and remaining silent until what he had to do was done.

In a word, I should have set this man down as one of the safest of men to be employed in that capacity, but for the circumstance that while he was speaking to me he twice broke off with a fallen colour, turned his face towards the little bell when it did not ring, opened the door of the hut (which was kept shut to exclude the unhealthy damp), and looked out towards the red light near the mouth of the tunnel. On both of those occasions, he came back to the fire with the inexplicable air upon him which I had remarked, without being able to define it, when we were so far asunder.

Said I, when I rose to leave him, 'You almost make me think that I have met with a contented man.'

(I am afraid I must acknowledge that I said it to lead him on.)

'I believe I used to be so,' he rejoined, in the low voice in which he had first spoken; 'but I am troubled, sir, I am troubled.'

He would have recalled the words if he could. He had said them, however, and I took them up quickly.

'With what? What is your trouble?'

'It is very difficult to impart, sir. It is very, very difficult to speak of. If ever you make me another visit, I will try to tell you.'

'But I expressly intend to make you another visit. Say, when shall it be?'

'I go off early in the morning, and I shall be on again at

ten tomorrow night, sir.'

'I will come at eleven.'

He thanked me, and went out at the door with me. 'I'll show my white light, sir,' he said, in his peculiar low voice, 'till you have found the way up. When you have found it, don't call out! And when you are at the top, don't call out!'

His manner seemed to make the place strike colder to me, but I said no more than, 'Very well.'

'And when you come down tomorrow night, don't call out! Let me ask you a parting question. What made you cry? "Halloa! Below there!" tonight?'

'Heaven knows,' said I. 'I cried something to that effect—'

'Not to that effect, sir. Those were the very words. I know them well.'

'Admit those were the very words. I said them, no doubt, because I saw you below.'

'For no other reason?'

'What other reason could I possibly have?'

'You had no feeling that they were conveyed to you in any supernatural way?'

'No.'

He wished me goodnight, and held up his light. I walked by the side of the down line of rails (with a very disagreeable sensation of a train coming behind me) until I found the path. It was easier to mount than to descend, and I got back to my inn without any adventure.

Punctual to my appointment, I placed my foot on the first notch of the zigzag next night, as the distant clocks were striking eleven. He was waiting for me at the bottom, with his white light on. 'I have not called out,' I said, when we came close together; 'may I speak now?' 'By all means, sir.' 'Goodnight, then, and here's my hand.' 'Goodnight, sir, and here's mine.' With that we walked side by side to his box, entered it, closed the door, and sat down by the fire.

'I have made up my mind, sir,' he began, bending forward as soon as we were seated, and speaking in a tone but a little above a whisper, 'that you shall not have to ask me twice what troubles me. I took you for someone else yesterday evening. That troubles me.'

'That mistake?'

'No. That someone else.'

'Who is it?'

'I don't know.'

'Like me?'

'I don't know. I never saw the face. The left arm is across the face, and the right arm is waved—violently waved. This way.'

I followed his action with my eyes, and it was the action of an arm gesticulating, with the utmost passion and vehemence, 'For God's sake, clear the way!'

'One moonlight night,' said the man, 'I was sitting here, when I heard a voice cry, 'Halloa! Below there!' I started up, looked from that door, and saw this Someone else standing by the red light near the tunnel, waving as I just now showed you. The voice seemed hoarse with shouting, and it cried, 'Look out! Look out!' And then again, 'Halloa! Below there! Look out!' I caught up my lamp, turned it on red, and ran towards the figure, calling, 'What's wrong? What has happened? Where?' It stood just outside the blackness of the tunnel. I advanced so close upon it that I wondered at its keeping the sleeve across its eyes. I ran right up at it, and had my hand stretched out to pull the sleeve away, when it was gone.'

'Into the tunnel?' said I.

'No. I ran on into the tunnel, five hundred yards. I stopped, and held my lamp above my head, and saw the figures of the measured distance, and saw the wet stains stealing down the walls and trickling through the arch. I ran out again faster than I had run in (for I had a mortal abhorrence of the place upon me), and I looked all round the red light with my own red light, and I went up the iron ladder to the gallery atop of it, and I came down again, and ran back here. I telegraphed both ways, 'An alarm has been given. Is anything wrong?' The answer came back, both ways, 'All well.''

Resisting the slow touch of a frozen finger tracing out my spine, I showed him how that this figure must be a deception of his sense of sight; and how that figures, originating in disease of the delicate nerves that minister to the functions of the eye, were known to have often troubled patients, some of whom had become conscious of the nature of their affliction, and had even proved it by experiments upon themselves. 'As to an imaginary cry,' said I, 'do but listen for a moment to the wind in this unnatural valley while we speak so low, and to the wild harp it makes of the telegraph wires.'

That was all very well, he returned, after we had sat listening for a while, and he ought to know something of the wind and the wires—he who so often passed long winter nights there, alone and watching. But he would beg to remark that he had not finished.

I asked his pardon, and he slowly added these words, touching my arm,

'Within six hours after the Appearance, the memorable accident on this line happened, and within ten hours the dead and wounded were brought along through the tunnel over the spot where the figure had stood.'

A disagreeable shudder crept over me, but I did my best against it. It was not to be denied, I rejoined, that this was a remarkable coincidence, calculated deeply to impress his mind. But it was unquestionable that remarkable coincidences did continually occur, and they must be taken into account in dealing with such a subject. Though to be sure I must admit, I added (for I thought I saw that he was going to bring the objection to bear upon me), men of common sense did not allow much for coincidences in making the ordinary calculations of life.

He again begged to remark that he had not finished.

I again begged his pardon for being betrayed into interruptions.

'This,' he said, again laying his hand upon my arm, and glancing over his shoulder with hollow eyes, 'was just a year ago. Six or seven months passed, and I had recovered from the surprise and shock, when one morning, as the day was breaking, I, standing at the door, looked towards the red light, and saw the spectre again.' He stopped, with a fixed look at me.

'Did it cry out?'

'No. It was silent.'

'Did it wave its arm?'

'No. It leaned against the shaft of the light, with both hands before the face. Like this.'

Once more I followed his action with my eyes. It was an action of mourning. I have seen such an attitude in stone figures on tombs.

'Did you go up to it?'

'I came in and sat down, partly to collect my thoughts, partly because it had turned me faint. When I went to the door again, daylight was above me, and the ghost was gone.'

'But nothing followed? Nothing came of this?'

He touched me on the arm with his forefinger twice or thrice giving a ghastly nod each time:-

'That very day, as a train came out of the tunnel, I noticed, at a carriage window on my side, what looked like a confusion of hands and heads, and something waved. I saw it just in time to signal the driver, Stop! He shut off, and put his brake on, but the train drifted past here a hundred and fifty yards or more. I ran after it, and, as I went along, heard terrible screams and cries. A beautiful young lady had died instantaneously in one of the compartments, and was brought in here, and laid down on this floor between us.'

Involuntarily I pushed my chair back, as I looked from the boards at which he pointed to himself.

'True, sir. True. Precisely as it happened, so I tell it to you.'

I could think of nothing to say, to any purpose, and my mouth was very dry. The wind and the wires took up the story with a long lamenting wail.

He resumed. 'Now, sir, mark this, and judge how my mind is troubled. The spectre came back a week ago. Ever since, it has been there, now and again, by fits and starts.'

'At the light?'

'At the Danger-light.'

'What does it seem to do?'

He repeated, if possible with increased passion and vehemence, that former gesticulation of, 'For God's sake, clear the way!'

Then he went on. 'I have no peace or rest for it. It calls to me, for many minutes together, in an agonized manner, 'Below there! Look out! Look out!' It stands waving to me. It rings my little bell—'

I caught at that. 'Did it ring your bell yesterday evening

when I was here, and you went to the door?'

'Twice.'

'Why, see,' said I, 'how your imagination misleads you. My eyes were on the bell, and my ears were open to the bell, and if I am a living man, it did NOT ring at those times. No, nor at any other time, except when it was rung in the natural course of physical things by the station communicating with you.'

He shook his head. 'I have never made a mistake as to that yet, sir. I have never confused the spectre's ring with the man's. The ghost's ring is a strange vibration in the bell that it derives from nothing else, and I have not asserted that the bell stirs to the eye. I don't wonder that you failed to hear it. But I heard it.'

'And did the spectre seem to be there, when you looked out?'

'It WAS there."

'Both times?'

He repeated firmly: 'Both times.'

'Will you come to the door with me, and look for it now?'

He bit his under lip as though he were somewhat unwilling, but arose. I opened the door, and stood on the step, while he stood in the doorway. There was the Danger-light. There was the dismal mouth of the tunnel. There were the high, wet stone walls of the cutting. There were the stars above them.

'Do you see it?' I asked him, taking particular note of his face. His eyes were prominent and strained, but not very much more so, perhaps, than my own had been when I had directed them earnestly towards the same spot.

'No,' he answered. 'It is not there.'

'Agreed,' said I.

We went in again, shut the door, and resumed our seats. I was thinking how best to improve this advantage, if it might be called one, when he took up the conversation in such a matter-of-course way, so assuming that there could be no serious question of fact between us, that I felt myself placed in the weakest of positions.

'By this time you will fully understand, sir,' he said, 'that what troubles me so dreadfully is the question, What does the spectre mean?'

I was not sure, I told him, that I did fully understand.

'What is its warning against?' he said, ruminating, with his eyes on the fire, and only by times turning them on me. 'What is the danger? Where is the danger? There is danger overhanging somewhere on the line. Some dreadful calamity will happen. It is not to be doubted this third time, after what has gone before. But surely this is a cruel haunting of me. What can I do?'

He pulled out his handkerchief, and wiped the drops from his heated forehead.

'If I telegraph Danger, on either side of me, or on both, I can give no reason for it,' he went on, wiping the palms of his hands. 'I should get into trouble, and do no good. They would think I was mad. This is the way it would work—Message: 'Danger! Take care!' Answer: 'What Danger? Where?' Message: 'Don't know. But, for God's sake, take care!' They would displace me. What else could they do?'

His pain of mind was most pitiable to see. It was the mental torture of a conscientious man, oppressed beyond endurance by an unintelligible responsibility involving life.

'When it first stood under the Danger-light,' he went on, putting his dark hair back from his head, and drawing his hands outward across and across his temples in an extremity of feverish distress, 'why not tell me where that accident was to happen—if it must happen? Why not tell me how it could be averted—if it could have been averted? When on its second coming it hid its face, why not tell me, instead, 'She is going to die. Let them keep her at home?' If it came, on those two occasions, only to show me that its warnings were true, and so to prepare me for the third, why not warn me plainly now? And I, Lord help me! A mere poor signal-man on this solitary station! Why not go to somebody with credit to be believed, and power to act?'

When I saw him in this state, I saw that for the poor man's sake, as well as for the public safety, what I had to do for the present time was to compose his mind. Therefore, setting aside all question of reality or unreality between us, I represented to him that whoever thoroughly discharged his duty must do well, and that at least it was his comfort that he understood his duty, though he did not understand these confounding Appearances. In this effort I succeeded far better than in the attempt to reason him out of his conviction. He became calm; the occupations incidental to his post as the night advanced began to make larger demands on his attention: and I left him at two in the morning. I had offered to stay through the night, but he would not hear of it.

That I more than once looked back at the red light as I ascended the pathway, that I did not like the red light, and that I should have slept but poorly if my bed had been under it, I see no reason to conceal. Nor did I like the two sequences of the accident and the dead girl. I see no reason to conceal that either.

But what ran most in my thoughts was the consideration how ought I to act, having become the recipient of this disclosure? I had proved the man to be intelligent, vigilant, painstaking, and exact; but how long might he remain so, in his state of mind? Though in a subordinate position, still he held a most important trust, and would I (for instance) like to stake my own life on the chances of his continuing to execute it with precision?

Unable to overcome a feeling that there would be something treacherous in my communicating what he had told me to his superiors in the Company, without first being plain with himself and proposing a middle course to him, I ultimately resolved to offer to accompany him (otherwise keeping his secret for the present) to the wisest medical practitioner we could hear of in those parts, and to take his opinion. A change in his time of duty would come round next night, he had apprised me, and he would be off an hour or two after sunrise, and on again soon after sunset. I had appointed to return accordingly.

Next evening was a lovely evening, and I walked out early to enjoy it. The sun was not yet quite down when I traversed the field-path near the top of the deep cutting. I would extend my walk for an hour, I said to myself, half an hour on and half an hour back, and it would then be time to go to my signal-man's box.

Before pursuing my stroll, I stepped to the brink, and mechanically looked down, from the point from which I had first seen him. I cannot describe the thrill that seized upon me, when, close at the mouth of the tunnel, I saw the appearance of a man, with his left sleeve across his eyes, passionately waving his right arm.

The nameless horror that oppressed me passed in a moment, for in a moment I saw that this appearance was of a man indeed, and that there was a little group of other men, standing at a short distance, to whom he seemed to be rehearsing the gesture he made. The Danger-light was not yet lighted. Against its shaft, a little low hut, entirely new to me, had been made of some wooden supports and tarpaulin. It looked no bigger than a bed.

With an irresistible sense that something was wrong—with

a flashing self-reproachful fear that fatal mischief had come of my leaving the man there, and causing no one to be sent to overlook or correct what he did—I descended the notched path with all the speed I could make.

'What is the matter?' I asked the men.

'Signal-man killed this morning, sir.'

'Not the man belonging to that box?'

'Yes, sir.'

'Not the man I know?'

'You will recognize him, sir, if you knew him,' said the man who spoke for the others, solemnly uncovering his own head, and raising an end of the tarpaulin, 'for his face is quite composed.'

'O, how did this happen, how did this happen?' I asked, turning from one to another as the hut closed in again.

'He was cut down by an engine, sir. No man in England knew his work better. But somehow he was not clear of the outer rail. It was just at broad day. He had struck the light, and had the lamp in his hand. As the engine came out of the tunnel, his back was towards her, and she cut him down. That man drove her, and was showing how it happened. Show the gentleman, Tom.'

The man, who wore a rough dark dress, stepped back to his former place at the mouth of the tunnel.

'Coming round the curve in the tunnel, sir,' he said, 'I saw him at the end, like as if I saw him down a perspective-glass. There was no time to check speed, and I knew him to be very careful. As he didn't seem to take heed of the whistle, I shut it off when we were running down upon him, and called to him as loud as I could call.'

'What did you say?'

'I said, 'Below there! Look out! Look out! For God's sake, clear the way!"

I started.

'Ah! it was a dreadful time, sir. I never left off calling to him. I put this arm before my eyes not to see, and I waved this arm to the last; but it was no use.'

Without prolonging the narrative to dwell on any one of its curious circumstances more than on any other, I may, in closing it, point out the coincidence that the warning of the Engine-Driver included, not only the words which the unfortunate Signal-man had repeated to me as haunting him, but also the words which I myself—not he—had attached, and that only in my own mind, to the gesticulation he had imitated.

DÉSIRÉE'S BABY

Kate Chopin

As the day was pleasant, Madame Valmondé drove over to L'Abri to see Désirée and the baby.

It made her laugh to think of Désirée with a baby. Why, it seemed but yesterday that Désirée was little more than a baby herself; when Monsieur in riding through the gateway of Valmondé had found her lying asleep in the shadow of the big stone pillar.

The little one awoke in his arms and began to cry for 'Dada.' That was as much as she could do or say. Some people thought she might have strayed there of her own accord, for she was of the toddling age. The prevailing belief was that she had been purposely left by a party of Texans, whose canvas-covered wagon, late in the day, had crossed the ferry that Coton Mais kept, just below the plantation. In time Madame Valmondé abandoned every speculation but the one that Désirée had been sent to her by a beneficent Providence to be the child of her affection, seeing that she was without child of the flesh. For the girl grew to be beautiful and gentle, affectionate and sincere—the idol of Valmondé.

It was no wonder, when she stood one day against the

stone pillar in whose shadow she had lain asleep, eighteen years before, that Armand Aubigny riding by and seeing her there, had fallen in love with her. That was the way all the Aubignys fell in love, as if struck by a pistol shot. The wonder was that he had not loved her before; for he had known her since his father brought him home from Paris, a boy of eight, after his mother died there. The passion that awoke in him that day, when he saw her at the gate, swept along like an avalanche, or like a prairie fire, or like anything that drives headlong over all obstacles.

Monsieur Valmonde grew practical and wanted things well considered: that is, the girl's obscure origin. Armand looked into her eyes and did not care. He was reminded that she was nameless. What did it matter about a name when he could give her one of the oldest and proudest in Louisiana? He ordered the corbeille from Paris, and contained himself with what patience he could until it arrived; then they were married.

Madame Valmonde had not seen Désirée and the baby for four weeks. When she reached L'Abri she shuddered at the first sight of it, as she always did. It was a sad looking place, which for many years had not known the gentle presence of a mistress, old Monsieur Aubigny having married and buried his wife in France, and she having loved her own land too well ever to leave it. The roof came down steep and black like a cowl, reaching out beyond the wide galleries that encircled the yellow stuccoed house. Big, solemn oaks grew close to it, and their thick-leaved, far-reaching branches shadowed it like a pall. Young Aubigny's rule was a strict one, too, and under it his negroes had forgotten how to be gay, as they had been during the old master's easy-going and indulgent lifetime.

The young mother was recovering slowly, and lay full length, in her soft white muslins and laces, upon a couch. The baby was beside her, upon her arm, where he had fallen asleep, at her breast. The yellow nurse woman sat beside a window fanning herself.

Madame Valmondé bent her portly figure over Désirée and kissed her, holding her an instant tenderly in her arms. Then she turned to the child.

'This is not the baby!' she exclaimed, in startled tones. French was the language spoken at Valmondé in those days.

'I knew you would be astonished,' laughed Désirée, 'at the way he has grown. The little *cochon de lait*! Look at his legs, mamma, and his hands and fingernails—real fingernails. Zandrine had to cut them this morning. Isn't it true, Zandrine?'

The woman bowed her turbaned head majestically, 'Mais si, Madame.'

'And the way he cries,' went on Désirée, 'is deafening. Armand heard him the other day as far away as La Blanche's cabin.'

Madame Valmondé had never removed her eyes from the child. She lifted it and walked with it over to the window that was lightest. She scanned the baby narrowly, then looked as searchingly at Zandrine, whose face was turned to gaze across the fields.

'Yes, the child has grown, has changed,' said Madame Valmondé, slowly, as she replaced it beside its mother. 'What does Armand say?'

Désirée's face became suffused with a glow that was happiness itself.

'Oh, Armand is the proudest father in the parish, I believe, chiefly because it is a boy, to bear his name; though he says not—that he would have loved a girl as well. But I know it isn't true. I know he says that to please me. And mamma,' she added, drawing Madame Valmondé's head down to her, and speaking in a whisper, 'he hasn't punished one of them—not one of them—since baby is born. Even Negrillon, who pretended to have burnt his leg that he might rest from work—he only laughed, and said Negrillon was a great scamp. Oh, mamma, I'm so happy; it frightens me.'

What Désirée said was true. Marriage, and later the birth of his son had softened Armand Aubigny's imperious and exacting nature greatly. This was what made the gentle Désirée so happy, for she loved him desperately. When he frowned she trembled, but loved him. When he smiled, she asked no greater blessing of God. But Armand's dark, handsome face had not often been disfigured by frowns since the day he fell in love with her.

When the baby was about three months old, Désirée awoke one day to the conviction that there was something in the air menacing her peace. It was at first too subtle to grasp. It had only been a disquieting suggestion; an air of mystery among the blacks; unexpected visits from far-off neighbours who could hardly account for their coming. Then a strange, an awful change in her husband's manner, which she dared not ask him to explain. When he spoke to her, it was with averted eyes, from which the old love-light seemed to have gone out. He absented himself from home; and when there, avoided her presence and that of her child, without excuse. And the very spirit of Satan seemed suddenly to take hold of him in his dealings with the slaves. Désirée was miserable enough to die.

She sat in her room, one hot afternoon, in her peignoir, listlessly drawing through her fingers the strands of her long, silky brown hair that hung about her shoulders. The baby, half naked, lay asleep upon her own great mahogany bed, that was like a sumptuous throne, with its satin-lined half-canopy. One of La Blanche's little quadroon boys—half naked too—stood fanning the child slowly with a fan of peacock feathers. Désirée's eyes had been fixed absently and sadly upon the baby, while she was striving to penetrate the threatening mist that she felt closing about her. She looked from her child to the boy who stood beside him, and back again; over and over. 'Ah!' It was a cry that she could not help; which she was not conscious of having uttered. The blood turned like ice in her veins, and a clammy moisture gathered upon her face.

She tried to speak to the little quadroon boy; but no sound would come, at first. When he heard his name uttered, he looked up, and his mistress was pointing to the door. He laid aside the great, soft fan, and obediently stole away, over the polished floor, on his bare tiptoes.

She stayed motionless, with gaze riveted upon her child, and her face the picture of fright.

Presently her husband entered the room, and without noticing her, went to a table and began to search among some papers which covered it.

'Armand,' she called to him, in a voice which must have stabbed him, if he was human. But he did not notice. 'Armand,' she said again. Then she rose and tottered towards him. 'Armand,' she panted once more, clutching his arm, 'look at our child. What does it mean? Tell me.'

He coldly but gently loosened her fingers from about his arm and thrust the hand away from him. 'Tell me what it means!' she cried despairingly.

'It means,' he answered lightly, 'that the child is not white; it means that you are not white.'

A quick conception of all that this accusation meant for

her nerved her with unwonted courage to deny it. 'It is a lie; it is not true, I am white! Look at my hair, it is brown; and my eyes are grey, Armand, you know they are grey. And my skin is fair,' seizing his wrist. 'Look at my hand; whiter than yours, Armand,' she laughed hysterically.

'As white as La Blanche's,' he returned cruelly; and went away leaving her alone with their child.

When she could hold a pen in her hand, she sent a despairing letter to Madame Valmondé.

'My mother, they tell me I am not white. Armand has told me I am not white. For God's sake tell them it is not true. You must know it is not true. I shall die. I must die. I cannot be so unhappy, and live.'

The answer that came was brief:

'My own Désirée: Come home to Valmondé; back to your mother who loves you. Come with your child.'

When the letter reached Désirée she went with it to her husband's study, and laid it open upon the desk before which he sat. She was like a stone image: silent, white, motionless after she placed it there.

In silence he ran his cold eyes over the written words.

He said nothing. 'Shall I go, Armand?' she asked in tones sharp with agonized suspense.

'Yes, go.'

'Do you want me to go?'

'Yes, I want you to go.'

He thought Almighty God had dealt cruelly and unjustly with him; and felt, somehow, that he was paying Him back in kind when he stabbed thus into his wife's soul. Moreover he no longer loved her, because of the unconscious injury she had brought upon his home and his name.

She turned away like one stunned by a blow, and walked slowly towards the door, hoping he would call her back.

'Goodbye, Armand,' she moaned.

He did not answer her. That was his last blow at fate.

Désirée went in search of her child. Zandrine was pacing the sombre gallery with it. She took the little one from the nurse's arms with no word of explanation, and descending the steps, walked away, under the live-oak branches.

It was an October afternoon; the sun was just sinking. Out in the still fields the negroes were picking cotton.

Désirée had not changed the thin white garment nor the slippers which she wore. Her hair was uncovered and the sun's rays brought a golden gleam from its brown meshes. She did not take the broad, beaten road which led to the far-off plantation of Valmonde. She walked across a deserted field, where the stubble bruised her tender feet, so delicately shod, and tore her thin gown to shreds.

She disappeared among the reeds and willows that grew thick along the banks of the deep, sluggish bayou; and she did not come back again.

Some weeks later there was a curious scene enacted at L'Abri. In the centre of the smoothly swept backyard was a great bonfire. Armand Aubigny sat in the wide hallway that commanded a view of the spectacle; and it was he who dealt out to a half dozen negroes the material which kept this fire ablaze.

A graceful cradle of willow, with all its dainty furbishings, was laid upon the pyre, which had already been fed with the richness of a priceless layette. Then there were silk gowns, and velvet and satin ones added to these; laces, too, and embroideries; bonnets and gloves; for the corbeille had been of rare quality.

The last thing to go was a tiny bundle of letters; innocent

little scribblings that Désirée had sent to him during the days of their espousal. There was the remnant of one back in the drawer from which he took them. But it was not Désirée's; it was part of an old letter from his mother to his father. He read it. She was thanking God for the blessing of her husband's love:

'But above all,' she wrote, 'night and day, I thank the good God for having so arranged our lives that our dear Armand will never know that his mother, who adores him, belongs to the race that is cursed with the brand of slavery.'

THE VAMPIRE

Sydney Horler

Until his death, quite recently, I used to visit at least once a week a Roman Catholic priest. The fact that I am a Protestant did nothing to shake our friendship. Father R—— was one of the finest characters I have ever known; he was capable of the broadest sympathies, and was, in the best sense of that frequently-abused term, 'a man of the world.' He was good enough to take considerable interest in my work as a novelist, and I often discussed plots and situations with him.

The story I am about to relate occurred about eighteen months ago—ten months before his illness. I was then writing my novel *The Curse of Doone*. In this story I made the villain taking advantage of a ghasty legend attached to an old manor-house in Devonshire and use it for his own ends.

Father R—— listened while I outlined the plot I had in mind, and then said, to my great surprise: 'Certain people may scoff because they will not allow themselves to believe that there is any credence in the vampire tradition.'

'Yes, that is so,' I parried; 'but, all the same, Bram Stoker stirred the public imagination with his "Dracula"—one of the most horrible and yet fascinating books ever written—and I am hoping that my public will extend to me the customary "author's licence."'

My friend nodded.

'Quite,' he replied. 'As a matter of fact,' he went on to say, 'I believe in vampires myself.'

'You do?' I felt the hair on the back of my neck commence to irritate. It is one thing to write about a horror, but quite another to begin to see it assume definite shape. 'Yes,' said Father R——'I am forced to believe in vampires for the very good but terrible reason that I have met one!'

I half-rose in my chair. There could be no questioning R——'s word, and yet.

'That, no doubt, my dear fellow,' he continued, 'may appear a very extraordinary statement to have made, and yet I assure you it is the truth. It happened many years ago and in another part of the country—exactly where I do not think I had better tell you.'

'But this is amazing! You say you actually met a vampire face to face?'

'And talked to him. Until now I have never mentioned the matter to a living soul apart from a brother priest.'

It was clearly an invitation to listen; I crammed tobacco into my pipe and leaned back in the chair on the opposite side of the crackling fire. I had heard that Truth was said to be stranger than fiction—but here I was about to have, it seemed, the strange experience of listening to my own most sensational imagining being hopelessly outdone by *fact*!

'The name of the small town does not matter' (Father R—— started); 'let it suffice it was in the West of England and was inhabited by a good many people of superior means. There was a large city seventy-five miles away and businessmen, when they retired, often came to—to wind up their lives. I was young and very happy there in my work until—But I am a little previous.

'I was on very friendly terms with a local doctor; he often used to come in and have a chat when he could spare the time. We used to try to thresh out many problems which later experience has convinced me are insoluble—in this world, at least.

'One night, he looked at me rather curiously,' I thought.

'"What do you think of that man, Farington?" he asked.

'Now, it was a curious fact that he should have made that inquiry at that exact moment, for by some subconscious means I happened to be thinking of this very person myself.

'The man who called himself "Joseph Farington" was a stranger who had recently come to settle in—. That circumstance alone would have caused comment, but when I say that he had bought the largest house on the hill overlooking the town on the south side (representing the best residential quarter) and had it furnished apparently regardless of cost by one of the famous London houses, that he sought to entertain a great deal but that no one seemed anxious to go twice to "The Gables." Well, there was "something funny" about Farington, it was whispered.

'I knew this, of course—the smallest fragment of gossip comes to a priest's ear—and so I hesitated before replying to the doctor's direct question.

'"Confess now, Father," said my companion, "you are like all the rest of us—you don't like the man! He has made me his medical attendant, but I wish to goodness he had chosen someone else. There's 'something funny' about him."

'"Something funny"—there it was again. As the doctor's words sounded in my ears I remembered Farington as I had last seen him walking up the main street with every other eye half-turned in his direction. He was a big-framed man, the essence of masculinity. He looked so robust that the thought came instinctively: This man will never die. He had a florid complexion; he walked with the elasticity of youth and his hair was jet black. Yet from remarks he had made the impression in—was that Farington must be at least sixty years of age.

"'Well, there's one thing, Sanders," I replied; "if appearances are anything to go by, Farington will not be giving you much trouble. The fellow looks as strong as an ox."

"'You haven't answered my question,' persisted the doctor. "Forget your cloth, Father, and tell me exactly what you think of Joseph Farington. Don't you agree that he is a man to give you the shudders?"

"'You—a doctor-talking about getting the shudders!" I gently scoffed because I did not want to give my real opinion of Joseph Farington.

"'I can't help it—I have an instinctive horror of the fellow. This afternoon I was called up to 'The Gables'. Farington, like ever so many of his ox-like kind, is really a bit of a hypochondriac. He thought there was something wrong with his heart, he said."

"'And was there?'

"'The man ought to live to a hundred! But, I tell you, Father, I hated having to be near the fellow, there's something uncanny about him. I felt frightened—yes, frightened—all the time I was in the house. I had to talk to someone about it and as you are the safest person in—I dropped in...You haven't said anything yourself, I notice."

"'I prefer to wait,' I replied. It seemed the safest answer.

'Two months after that conversation with Sanders, not only me—but the whole of the country was startled and horrified by a terrible crime. A girl of eighteen, the belle of the district, was found dead in a field. Her face, in life so beautiful, was revolting in death because of the expression of dreadful horror it held.

'The poor girl had been murdered—but in a manner which sent shudders of fear racing up and down people's spines... There was a great hole in the throat, as though a beast of the jungle had attacked...

'It is not difficult to say how suspicion for this fiendish crime first started to fasten itself on Joseph Farington, preposterous as the statement may seem. Although he had gone out of his way to become sociable, the man had made no real friends. Sanders, although a clever doctor, was not the most tactful of men and there is no doubt that his refusal to visit Farington professionally—he had hinted as much on the night of his visit to me, you will remember—got noised about. In any case, public opinion was strongly roused; without a shred of direct evidence to go upon, people began to talk of Farington as being the actual murderer. There was some talk among the wild young spirits of setting fire to "The Gables" one night, and burning Farington in his bed.

'It was whilst this feeling was at its height that, very unwillingly, as you may imagine, I was brought into the affair. I received a note from Farington asking me to dine with him one night.

'"I have something on my mind which I wish to talk over with you; so please do not fail me."

'These were the concluding words of the letter.

'Such an appeal could not be ignored by a man of religion and so I replied accepting.

'Farington was a good host; the food was excellent; on the surface there was nothing wrong. But—and here is the curious part–from the moment I faced the man I knew there was something wrong. I had the same uneasiness as Sanders, the doctor: *I felt afraid.* The man had an aura of evil; he was possessed of some devilish force or quality which chilled me to the marrow.

'I did my best to hide my discomfiture, but when, after dinner, Farington began to speak about the murder of that poor, innocent girl, this feeling increased. And at once the terrible truth leaped into my mind: I knew it was Farington who had done this crime: the man was a monster!

'Calling upon all my strength, I challenged him.

'"You wished to see me tonight for the purpose of easing your soul of a terrible burden," I said; "you cannot deny that it was you who killed that unfortunate girl."

'"Yes," he replied slowly, "that is the truth. I killed the girl. The demon which possesses me forced me to do it. But you, as a priest, must hold this confession sacred—you must preserve it as a secret. Give me a few more hours; then I will decide myself what to do."

'I left shortly afterwards. The man would not say anything more.

'"Give me a few hours," he repeated.

'That night I had a horrible dream. I felt I was suffocating. Scarcely able to breathe, I rushed to the window, pulled it open and then fell senseless to the floor. The next thing I remember was Dr Sanders—who had been summoned by my faithful housekeeper—bending over me.

'"What happened?" he asked. "You had a look on your face as though you had been staring into hell."

'"So I had," I replied.

'"Had it anything to do with Farington?" he asked bluntly.

'"Sanders," and I clutched him by the arm in the intensity

of my feeling, "does such a monstrosity as a vampire exist nowadays? Tell me, I implore you!"

'The good fellow forced me to take another nip of brandy before he would reply.

'Then he put a question himself.

'"Why do you ask that?" he said.

'"It sounds incredible—and I hope I really dreamed it—but I fainted tonight because I saw—or imagined I saw—the man Farington flying past the window that I had just opened."

'"I am not surprised," he nodded. "Ever since I examined the mutilated body of that poor girl I came to the conclusion that she had come to her death through some terrible abnormality.

"Although we hear practically nothing about vampirism nowadays," he continued, "that is not to say that ghoulish spirits do not still take up their abode in a living man or woman, thus conferring upon them supernatural powers. What form was the shape you thought you saw?"

'"It was like a huge bat," I replied shuddering.

'"Tomorrow," said Sanders determinedly, "I'm going to London to see Scotland Yard. They may laugh at me at first, but—"

'Scotland Yard did not laugh. But criminals with supernatural powers were rather out of their line, and, besides, as they told Sanders, they had to have proof before they could convict Farington. Even my testimony—had I dared to break my priestly pledge, which, of course, I couldn't in any circumstances do—would not have been sufficient.

'Farington solved the terrible problem by committing suicide. He was found in bed with a bullet wound in his head.

'But, according to Sanders, only the body is dead—the vile spirit is roaming free, looking for another human habitation.

'God help its luckless victim.'

EYES OF THE CAT

Ruskin Bond

Her eyes seemed flecked with gold when the sun was on them. And as the sun set over the mountains, drawing a deep red wound across the sky, there was more than gold in Kiran's eyes. There was anger; for she had been cut to the quick by some remarks her teacher had made—the culmination of weeks of insults and taunts.

Kiran was poorer than most of the girls in her class and could not afford the tuitions that had become almost obligatory if one was to pass and be promoted. 'You'll have to spend another year in the ninth,' said Madam. 'And if you don't like that, you can find another school—a school where it won't matter if your blouse is torn and your tunic is old and your shoes are falling apart.' Madam had shown her large teeth in what was supposed to be a good-natured smile, and all the girls had tittered dutifully. Sycophancy had become part of the curriculum in Madam's private academy for girls.

On the way home in the gathering gloom, Kiran's two companions commiserated with her.

'She's a mean old thing,' said Aarti. 'She doesn't care for anyone but herself.'

'Her laugh reminds me of a donkey braying,' said Sunita, who was more forthright.

But Kiran wasn't really listening. Her eyes were fixed on some point in the far distance, where the pines stood in silhouette against a night sky that was growing brighter every moment. The moon was rising, a full moon, a moon that meant something very special to Kiran, that made her blood tingle and her skin prickle and her hair glow and send out sparks. Her steps seemed to grow lighter, her limbs more sinewy as she moved gracefully, softly over the mountain path.

Abruptly she left her companions at a fork in the road.

'I'm taking the short cut through the forest,' she said.

Her friends were used to her sudden whims. They knew she was not afraid of being alone in the dark. But Kiran's moods made them feel a little nervous, and now, holding hands, they hurried home along the open road.

The short cut took Kiran through the dark oak forest. The crooked, tormented branches of the oaks threw twisted shadows across the path. A jackal howled at the moon; a nightjar called from urgency, and her breath came in short, sharp gasps. Bright moonlight bathed the hillside when she reached her home on the outskirts of the village.

Refusing her dinner, she went straight to her small room and flung the window open. Moonbeams crept over the windowsill and over her arms which were already covered with golden hair. Her strong nails had shredded the rotten wood of the windowsill.

Tail swishing and ears pricked, the tawny leopard came swiftly out of the window, crossed the open field behind the house, and melted into the shadows.

A little later it padded silently through the forest.

Although the moon shone brightly on the tin-roofed town, the leopard knew where the shadows were deepest and merged beautifully with them. An occasional intake of breath, which resulted in a short rasping cough, was the only sound it made.

Madam was returning from dinner at a ladies' club, called the Kitten Club as a sort of foil to the husbands' club affiliations. There were still a few people in the street, and while no one could help noticing Madam, who had the contours of a steam-roller, none saw or heard the predator who had slipped down a side alley and reached the steps of the teacher's house. It sat there silently, waiting with all the patience of an obedient schoolgirl.

When Madam saw the leopard on her steps, she dropped her handbag and opened her mouth to scream; but her voice would not materialize. Nor would her tongue ever be used again, either to savour chicken biryani or to pour scorn upon her pupils, for the leopard had sprung at her throat, broken her neck, and dragged her into the bushes.

In the morning, when Aarti and Sunita set out for school, they stopped as usual at Kiran's cottage and called out to her.

Kiran was sitting in the sun, combing her long black hair.

'Aren't you coming to school today, Kiran?' asked the girls.

'No, I won't bother to go today,' said Kiran. She felt lazy, but pleased with herself, like a contented cat.

'Madam won't be pleased,' said Aarti. 'Shall we tell her you're sick?'

'It won't be necessary,' said Kiran, and gave them one of her mysterious smiles. 'I'm sure it's going to be a holiday.'

THE STATEMENT OF RANDOLPH CARTER

H.P. Lovecraft

I repeat to you, gentlemen, that your inquisition is fruitless. Detain me here forever if you will; confine or execute me if you must have a victim to propitiate the illusion you call justice; but I can say no more than I have said already. Everything that I can remember, I have told with perfect candour. Nothing has been distorted or concealed, and if anything remains vague, it is only because of the dark cloud which has come over my mind—that cloud and the nebulous nature of the horrors which brought it upon me.

Again I say, I do not know what has become of Harley Warren; though I think—almost hope—that he is in peaceful oblivion, if there be anywhere so blessed a thing. It is true that I have for five years been his closest friend, and a partial sharer of his terrible researches into the unknown. I will not deny, though my memory is uncertain and indistinct, that this witness of yours may have seen us together as he says, on the Gainesville pike, walking toward Big Cypress Swamp, at half past eleven on that awful night. That we bore electric lanterns, spades, and a curious coil of wire with attached instruments, I will even affirm; for these things all played a part in the single hideous scene which remains burned into my shaken recollection. But of what followed, and of the reason I was found alone and dazed on the edge of the swamp next morning, I must insist that I know nothing save what I have told you over and over again. You say to me that there is nothing in the swamp or near it which could form the setting of that frightful episode. I reply that I know nothing beyond what I saw. Vision or nightmare it may have been—vision or nightmare I fervently hope it was— yet it is all that my mind retains of what took place in those shocking hours after we left the sight of men. And why Harley Warren did not return, he or his shade—or some nameless thing I cannot describe—alone can tell.

As I have said before, the weird studies of Harley Warren were well known to me, and to some extent shared by me. Of his vast collection of strange, rare books on forbidden subjects I have read all that are written in the languages of which I am master; but these are few as compared with those in languages I cannot understand. Most, I believe, are in Arabic; and the fiend-inspired book which brought on the end—the book which he carried in his pocket out of the world—was written in characters whose like I never saw elsewhere. Warren would never tell me just what was in that book. As to the nature of our studies— must I say again that I no longer retain full comprehension? It seems to me rather merciful that I do not, for they were terrible studies, which I pursued more through reluctant fascination than through actual inclination. Warren always dominated me, and sometimes I feared him. I remember how I shuddered at his facial expression on the night before the awful happening, when he talked so incessantly of his theory, why certain corpses never decay, but rest firm and fat in their tombs for a thousand years. But I do not fear him now, for I suspect that he has known horrors beyond my ken. Now I fear for him.

Once more I say that I have no clear idea of our object on that night. Certainly, it had much to do with something in the book which Warren carried with him—that ancient book in undecipherable characters which had come to him from India a month before—but I swear I do not know what it was that we expected to find. Your witness says he saw us at half past eleven on the Gainesville pike, headed for Big Cypress Swamp. This is probably true, but I have no distinct memory of it. The picture seared into my soul is of one scene only, and the hour must have been long after midnight; for a waning crescent moon was high in the vaporous heavens.

The place was an ancient cemetery; so ancient that I trembled at the manifold signs of immemorial years. It was in a deep, damp hollow, overgrown with rank grass, moss, and curious creeping weeds, and filled with a vague stench which my idle fancy associated absurdly with rotting stone. On every hand were the signs of neglect and decrepitude, and I seemed haunted by the notion that Warren and I were the first living creatures to invade a lethal silence of centuries. Over the valley's rim a wan, waning crescent moon peered through the noisome vapours that seemed to emanate from unheard-of catacombs, and by its feeble, wavering beams I could distinguish a repellent array of antique slabs, urns, cenotaphs, and mausolean facades; all crumbling, moss-grown, and moisture-stained, and partly concealed by the gross luxuriance of the unhealthy vegetation. My first vivid impression of my own presence in this terrible necropolis concerns the act of pausing with Warren before a certain half-obliterated sepulchre, and of throwing down some burdens which we seemed to have been carrying. I now observed that I had with me an electric lantern and two spades, whilst my companion was supplied with a similar lantern and a portable telephone outfit. No word was uttered, for the spot and the task seemed known to us; and without delay we seized our spades and commenced to clear away the grass, weeds, and drifted earth from the flat, archaic mortuary. After uncovering the entire surface, which consisted of three immense granite slabs, we stepped back some distance to survey the charnel scene; and Warren appeared to make some mental calculations. Then he returned to the sepulchre, and using his spade as a lever, sought to pry up the slab lying nearest to a stony ruin which may have been a monument in its day. He did not succeed, and motioned to me to come to his assistance. Finally our combined strength loosened the stone, which we raised and tipped to one side.

The removal of the slab revealed a black aperture, from which rushed an effluence of miasmal gases so nauseous that we started back in horror. After an interval, however, we approached the pit again, and found the exhalations less unbearable. Our lanterns disclosed the top of a flight of stone steps, dripping with some detestable ichor of the inner earth, and bordered by moist walls encrusted with nitre. And now for the first time my memory records verbal discourse, Warren addressing me at length in his mellow tenor voice; a voice singularly unperturbed by our awesome surroundings.

'I'm sorry to have to ask you to stay on the surface,' he said, 'but it would be a crime to let anyone with your frail nerves go down there. You can't imagine, even from what you have read and from what I've told you, the things I shall have to see and do. It's fiendish work, Carter, and I doubt if any man without ironclad sensibilities could ever see it through and come up alive and sane. I don't wish to offend you, and heaven knows I'd be glad enough to have you with me; but the responsibility is in a certain sense mine, and I couldn't drag a bundle of nerves like you down to probable death or madness. I tell you, you can't imagine what the thing is really like! But I promise to keep you informed over the telephone of every move—you see I've enough wire here to reach to the centre of the earth and back!'

I can still hear, in memory, those coolly spoken words; and I can still remember my remonstrances. I seemed desperately anxious to accompany my friend into those sepulchral depths, yet he proved inflexibly obdurate. At one time he threatened to abandon the expedition if I remained insistent; a threat which proved effective, since he alone held the key to the thing. All this I can still remember, though I no longer know what manner of thing we sought. After he had secured my reluctant acquiescence in his design, Warren picked up the reel of wire and adjusted the instruments. At his nod I took one of the latter and seated myself upon an aged, discoloured gravestone close by the newly uncovered aperture. Then he shook my hand, shouldered the coil of wire, and disappeared within that indescribable ossuary. For a moment I kept sight of the glow of his lantern, and heard the rustle of the wire as he laid it down after him; but the glow soon disappeared abruptly, as if a turn in the stone staircase had been encountered, and the sound died away almost as quickly. I was alone, yet bound to the unknown depths by those magic strands whose insulated surface lay green beneath the struggling beams of that waning crescent moon.

In the lone silence of that hoary and deserted city of the dead, my mind conceived the most ghastly fantasies and illusions; and the grotesque shrines and monoliths seemed to assume a hideous personality—a half-sentience. Amorphous shadows seemed to lurk in the darker recesses of the weed-choked hollow and to flit as in some blasphemous ceremonial procession past the portals of the mouldering tombs in the hillside; shadows which could not have been cast by that pallid, peering crescent moon. I constantly consulted my watch by the light of my electric lantern, and listened with feverish anxiety at the receiver of the telephone; but for more than a quarter of an hour heard nothing. Then a faint clicking came from the instrument, and I called down to my friend in a tense voice. Apprehensive as I was, I was nevertheless unprepared for the words which came up from that uncanny vault in accents more alarmed and quivering than any I had heard before from Harley Warren. He who had so calmly left me a little while previously, now called from below in a shaky whisper more portentous than the loudest shriek:

'God! If you could see what I am seeing!'

I could not answer. Speechless, I could only wait. Then came the frenzied tones again:

'Carter, it's terrible—monstrous—unbelievable!'

This time my voice did not fail me, and I poured into the transmitter a flood of excited questions. Terrified, I continued to repeat, 'Warren, what is it? What is it?'

Once more came the voice of my friend, still hoarse with fear, and now apparently tinged with despair:

'I can't tell you, Carter! It's too utterly beyond thought—I dare not tell you—no man could know it and live—Great God! I never dreamed of this!' Stillness again, save for my now incoherent torrent of shuddering inquiry. Then the voice of Warren in a pitch of wilder consternation:

'Carter! For the love of God, put back the slab and get out

of this if you can! Quick!—Leave everything else and make for the outside—it's your only chance! Do as I say, and don't ask me to explain!'

I heard, yet was able only to repeat my frantic questions. Around me were the tombs and the darkness and the shadows; below me, some peril beyond the radius of the human imagination. But my friend was in greater danger than I, and through my fear I felt a vague resentment that he should deem me capable of deserting him under such circumstances. More clicking, and after a pause a piteous cry from Warren:

'Beat it! For God's sake, put back the slab and beat it, Carter!'

Something in the boyish slang of my evidently stricken companion unleashed my faculties. I formed and shouted a resolution, 'Warren, brace up! I'm coming down!' But at this offer the tone of my auditor changed to a scream of utter despair:

'Don't! You can't understand! It's too late—and my own fault. Put back the slab and run—there's nothing else you or anyone can do now!' The tone changed again, this time acquiring a softer quality, as of hopeless resignation. Yet it remained tense through anxiety for me.

'Quick—before it's too late!' I tried not to heed him; tried to break through the paralysis which held me, and to fulfil my vow to rush down to his aid. But his next whisper found me still held inert in the chains of stark horror.

'Carter—hurry! It's no use—you must go—better one than two—the slab—' A pause, more clicking, then the faint voice of Warren:

'Nearly over now—don't make it harder—cover up those damned steps and run for your life—you're losing time. So long, Carter—won't see you again.' Here Warren's whisper swelled into a cry; a cry that gradually rose to a shriek fraught with all the horror of the ages—

'Curse these hellish things—legions—My God! Beat it! Beat it! Beat it!'

After that was silence. I know not how many interminable aeons I sat stupefied; whispering, muttering, calling, screaming into that telephone. Over and over again through those aeons I whispered and muttered, called, shouted, and screamed, 'Warren! Warren! Answer me—are you there?'

And then there came to me the crowning horror of all—the unbelievable, unthinkable, almost unmentionable thing. I have said that aeons seemed to elapse after Warren shrieked forth his last despairing warning, and that only my own cries now broke the hideous silence. But after a while there was a further clicking in the receiver, and I strained my ears to listen. Again I called down, 'Warren, are you there?', and in answer heard the thing which has brought this cloud over my mind. I do not try, gentlemen, to account for that thing—that voice—nor can I venture to describe it in detail, since the first words took away my consciousness and created a mental blank which reaches to the time of my awakening in the hospital. Shall I say that the voice was deep; hollow; gelatinous; remote; unearthly; inhuman; disembodied? What shall I say? It was the end of my experience, and is the end of my story. I heard it, and knew no more. Heard it as I sat petrified in that unknown cemetery in the hollow, amidst the crumbling stones and the falling tombs, the rank vegetation and the miasmal vapours. Heard it well up from the innermost depths of that damnable open sepulchre as I watched amorphous, necrophagous shadows dance beneath an accursed waning moon. And this is what it said:

'YOU FOOL, WARREN IS DEAD!'

THE STORY OF MUHAMMAD DIN

Rudyard Kipling

> *Who is the happy man? He that sees in his own house at home, little children crowned with dust, leaping and falling and crying.*
> —Munichandra, translated by Professor Peterson

The polo-ball was an old one, scarred, chipped, and dinted. It stood on the mantelpiece among the pipe-stems which Imam Din, khitmatgar, was cleaning for me.

'Does the Heaven-born want this ball?' said Imam Din, deferentially.

The Heaven-born set no particular store by it; but of what use was a polo-ball to a khitmatgar?

'By your Honour's favour, I have a little son. He has seen this ball, and desires it to play with. I do not want it for myself.'

No one would for an instant accuse portly old Imam Din of wanting to play with polo-balls. He carried out the battered thing into the veranda; and there followed a hurricane of joyful squeaks, a patter of small feet, and the thud-thud-thud of the ball rolling along the ground. Evidently the little son had been waiting outside the door to secure his treasure. But how had he managed to see that polo-ball?

Next day, coming back from office half an hour earlier than usual, I was aware of a small figure in the dining room—a tiny, plump figure in a ridiculously inadequate shirt which came, perhaps, halfway down the tubby stomach. It wandered round the room, thumb in mouth, crooning to itself as it took stock of the pictures. Undoubtedly this was the 'little son.'

He had no business in my room, of course; but was so deeply absorbed in his discoveries that he never noticed me in the doorway. I stepped into the room and startled him nearly into a fit. He sat down on the ground with a gasp. His eyes opened, and his mouth followed suit. I knew what was coming, and fled, followed by a long, dry howl which reached the servants' quarters far more quickly than any command of mine had ever done. In ten seconds Imam Din was in the dining room. Then despairing sobs arose, and I returned to find Imam Din admonishing the small sinner who was using most of his shirt as a handkerchief.

'This boy,' said Imam Din, judicially, 'is a budmash—a big budmash. He will, without doubt, go to the jail-khana for his behaviour.' Renewed yells from the penitent, and an elaborate apology to myself from Imam Din.

'Tell the baby,' said I, 'that the Sahib is not angry, and take him away.' Imam Din conveyed my forgiveness to the offender, who had now gathered all his shirt round his neck, stringwise, and the yell subsided into a sob. The two set off for the door. 'His name,' said Imam Din, as though the name were part of the crime, 'is Muhammad Din, and he is a budmash.' Freed from present danger, Muhammad Din turned round in his father's arms, and said gravely, 'It is true that my name is Muhammad

Din, Tahib, but I am not a budmash. I am a man!'

From that day dated my acquaintance with Muhammad Din. Never again did he come into my dining room, but on the neutral ground of the garden, we greeted each other with much state, though our conversation was confined to 'Talaam, Tahib' from his side, and 'Salaam, Muhammad Din' from mine. Daily on my return from office, the little white shirt, and the fat little body used to rise from the shade of the creeper-covered trellis where they had been hid; and daily I checked my horse here, that my salutation might not be slurred over or given unseemly.

Muhammad Din never had any companions. He used to trot about the compound, in and out of the castor-oil bushes, on mysterious errands of his own. One day I stumbled upon some of his handiwork far down the grounds. He had half buried the polo-ball in dust, and stuck six shriveled old marigold flowers in a circle round it.

Outside that circle again was a rude square, traced out in bits of red brick alternating with fragments of broken china; the whole bounded by a little bank of dust. The water-man from the well-curb put in a plea for the small architect, saying that it was only the play of a baby and did not much disfigure my garden.

Heaven knows that I had no intention of touching the child's work then or later; but, that evening, a stroll through the garden brought me unawares full on it; so that I trampled, before I knew, marigold-heads, dust-bank, and fragments of broken soap-dish into confusion past all hope of mending. Next morning, I came upon Muhammad Din crying softly to himself over the ruin I had wrought. Someone had cruelly told him that the Sahib was very angry with him for spoiling the garden, and had scattered his rubbish, using bad language the while. Muhammad Din laboured for an hour at effacing every trace of the dust-bank and pottery fragments, and it was with a tearful and apologetic face that he said 'Talaam, Tahib,' when I came home from office. A hasty inquiry resulted in Imam Din informing Muhammad Din that, by my singular favour, he was permitted to disport himself as he pleased. Whereat the child took heart and fell to tracing the ground-plan of an edifice which was to eclipse the marigold-polo-ball creation.

For some months, the chubby little eccentricity revolved in his humble orbit among the castor-oil bushes and in the dust; always fashioning magnificent palaces from stale flowers thrown away by the bearer, smooth water-worn pebbles, bits of broken glass, and feathers pulled, I fancy, from my fowls—always alone, and always crooning to himself.

A gaily-spotted seashell was dropped one day close to the last of his little buildings; and I looked that Muhammad Din should build something more than ordinarily splendid on the strength of it. Nor was I disappointed. He meditated for the better part of an hour, and his crooning rose to a jubilant song. Then he began tracing in the dust. It would certainly be a wondrous palace, this one, for it was two yards long and a yard broad in ground plan. But the palace was never completed.

Next day there was no Muhammad Din at the head of the carriage-drive, and no 'Talaam, Tahib' to welcome my return. I had grown accustomed to the greeting, and its omission troubled me. Next day Imam Din told me that the child was suffering slightly from fever and needed quinine. He got the medicine, and an English Doctor.

'They have no stamina, these brats,' said the Doctor, as he left Imam Din's quarters.

A week later, though I would have given much to have

avoided it, I met on the road to the Mussulman burying-ground Imam Din, accompanied by one other friend, carrying in his arms, wrapped in a white cloth, all that was left of little Muhammad Din.

NIGHT OF THE MILLENNIUM

Ruskin Bond

Jackals howled dismally, foraging for bones and offal down in the khud below the butcher's shop. Pasand was unperturbed by the sound. A robust young computer whiz-kid and patriotic multinational, he prided himself on being above and beyond all superstitious fears of the unknown. In his lexicon, the unknown was just something that was waiting to be discovered. Hence this walk past the old cemetery late at night.

Midnight would see the new millennium in. The year 2000 beckoned, full of bright prospects for well-heeled young men like Pasand. True, there were millions-soon to be over a billion—sweating it out in the heat and dust of the plains below, scraping together a meagre living for themselves and their sprawling families. Not for them the advantages of a public school education, three cars in the garage, and a bank account in Bermuda. Ah well, mused Pasand, not everyone could have the brains and good luck, as well as inherited family wealth of course, that had made life so pleasant and promising for him. This was going to be the century in which the smart-asses would get to the top and all other varieties of asses would sink to the bottom. It was important to have a ruling elite, according to his philosophy; only then could slaves prosper!

He looked at his watch. It was just past midnight. He had eaten well, and he was enjoying his little walk along the lonely winding road which took him past the houses of the rich and famous, the Lals, the Banerjees, the Kapoors, the Ramchandanis—he was as good as any of them! Better, in fact. He was approaching his own personal Everest, while they had reached theirs and were on the downward slope, or so he presumed.

Here was the cemetery with its broken old tombstones, some of them dating from a hundred and fifty years ago: pathetic reminders of a once-powerful empire, now reduced to dust and crumbling monuments. Here lay colonels and magistrates, merchants and memsahibs, and many small children; fragile lives which had been snuffed out in more turbulent times. To Pasand, they were losers, all of them. He had nothing but contempt for those who hadn't been able to hang on to their power and glory. No lost empires for him!

The road here was very dark, for the trees grew thick on the northern slopes. Pasand felt a twinge of nervousness, but he was reassured by the feel of the cellphone in his pocket. He could always summon his driver or his armed bodyguard to come and pick him up.

The moon had risen over Nag Tibba, and the graves stood out in serried rows, as though forming a guard of honour for this modern knight in T-shirt and designer jeans. Through the deodars he saw a faint light on the perimeter of the cemetery. Here, he had learnt from one of his chamchas, lived a widow with a brood of small children. Although in poor health, she was still young and comely, and known to be lavish with her favours to those who were generous with their purses; for she needed the money for her hungry family.

She was also a little mad, they said, and preferred to sleep in one of the old domed tombs rather than in the quarters provided for her late husband, who had been the caretaker.

This did not bother Pasand. He was in search of sensual pleasure, not romance. And right now he felt an urgent need to exert his dominance over someone, preferably a woman, for he had to prove his manhood in some way. So far, most young women had shied away from his vainglorious and clumsy approach.

This woman wasn't young. She was in her late thirties, and poverty, malnutrition and ill-use had made her look much older. But there were vestiges of beauty in her smouldering eyes and sinewy limbs. Her gypsy blood must have had something to do with it. Her teeth gleamed in the darkness as she smiled at Pasand and invited him into her boudoir—the spacious tomb that she favoured most.

Pasand had no time for tender love-play. Clumsily he clawed at her breasts but found they were not much larger than his own. He tore at her already tattered clothes, pressed his mouth hungrily to her dry lips. She made no attempt to resist. He had his way. Then, while he lay supine across the cold damp slab of a grave that covered the remains of some long-dead warrior, she leaned over him and bit him on the cheek and neck.

He cried out in pain and astonishment, and tried to sit up. But a number of hands, small but strong, thrust him back against the tombstone. Small mouths, sharp teeth, pressed against his flesh. Muddy fingers tore at his clothes. Those young teeth bit-and bit again. His screams mingled with the cries of the jackals.

'Patience, my children, patience,' crooned the woman. 'There is more than enough for all of you.'

They feasted.

Down in the ravine, the jackals started howling again, awaiting their turn. The bones would be theirs. Only the cellphone would be rejected.